GUILT IN INNOCENCE

A TALE OF THE SCATTERED EARTH

BY KEITH R. A. DeCANDIDO

FOLAMI BROADCAST HER THOUGHTS: *WAR Chief Tobi, clear out.*

I can stop the rest of the Eso, but I can't do it with Rufiji Company underfoot. Get to the drops and get back to L'owuro.

Tobi's voice sounded in Folami's earpiece, a method of communication far less secure. "Back to the drops? We can't—"

War Chief, if you don't do this, the rest of Rufiji will die. Sound the retreat!

Reluctantly, Tobi gave the order. Four cavalry lay down covering fire while the rest of the survivors of Rufiji retreated to the dropships.

Only one tree was still standing in the park, a thick, gnarled oak. Folami ran toward it after the drops took off, shooting her Bayo indiscriminately behind her to keep the Eso still chasing her at a distance. Nimbly, she climbed up as high as she could, the high ground giving her precious moments to collect herself. The rebels would be able to climb up after her, but soon, that wouldn't be an issue.

Because either her plan would work, or she'd be dead.

She took three deep breaths through her nose, exhaling through her mouth.

Two Eso started clambering up the twisted trunk of the oak, heading right for her.

She let out the most primal of screams.

THIS ONE'S FOR MARCO

ACKNOWLEDGMENTS

PRIMARY THANKS OBVIOUSLY HAVE TO go to Aaron Rosenberg, Steve Savile, and David Niall Wilson, the demiurges behind The Scattered Earth, who were kind enough to invite me to play in their sandbox.

Secondary thanks go, oddly, to the 1998/1999 television show *Young Hercules* and former Simon & Schuster editor Anne Greenberg, who hired me to write two novels based on that show. My second YH book, *The Ares Alliance*, involved Yoruba mythology (the plot revolved around a bit of a spat between Ares and Ogun), and sparked my interest in such, which led to the basis of the Olodumare Hegemony.

Speaking of which, the people of this novel—the Olodumare Hegemony and the fallen Oyo Empire—are very loosely based on the Yoruba people of the western part of Africa on Earth. However, we are also very far from the present day (in more ways than one), and any differences in traditions and culture should be attributed to that and author's choice.

Other helpful folks for various and sundry reasons include Jaime Costas, Laura Anne Gilman, Gerard Houarner, Neal Levin, Dale Mazur, Marco Palmieri, Tina Randleman, Wrenn Simms, and, of course, GraceAnne Andreassi DeCandido, a.k.a., The Mom.

Finally, thanks to them that live with me—human, canine, and feline—for support and wonderfulness, always.

As there is guilt in innocence, there is innocence in guilt.

—Yoruba proverb

CHAPTER ONE
Oshun

THE ESO SWUNG ITS DEADLY claw at Folami's head.

The sharp point was a nanosecond away from cutting through her protective face mask and her skull when the claw suddenly changed direction, whipping past her. Folami felt a whisper of air on her cheek, heard the whistle of the claw slicing through the air by her ear.

After telekinetically shoving the claw aside, Folami stared fiercely into her foe's eyes. Much of the Eso's body had been genetically altered: skin to a chitinous substance, fingers to rock-hard bone claws, a prehensile tail, all body hair removed.

But the eyes remained human.

Within a second of Folami's making eye contact with the Eso, her foe fell to the ground, dead, unnatural tail writhing desperately and mindlessly in the dirt, claws reaching upward, dead eyes gazing blindly upon Kaduna Township's dismal night sky.

She had used her mind to destroy his.

The battle was happening in what had once been a public park, located near the smoking ruins of what had been a refinery owned and operated by the Kaduna Mining Corporate. Most of the trees had been leveled and the grass scorched by the refinery explosion that had necessitated the arrival of Rufiji Cavalry Company, to which Folami had been assigned. Worse, it had rained recently, and the ground was muddy and hard to gain purchase on.

That was the tenth Eso that Folami had killed, and she was barely making a dent in their numbers. However, it was more than had been managed by War Chief Tobi and the rest of Rufiji.

At least the gas is finally starting to clear, she thought, looking up dolefully. From the moment they'd arrived at Oshun, there'd been a green miasma choking the air thanks to the refinery explosion.

Looking down at the Eso she'd mindblasted, a small part of Folami felt pity. The Eso were human once, but the last remnants of the fallen Oyo Empire, which continued to fight against the Olodumare Hegemony, had tampered with them, mutating them from human beings into killing machines with no memory of their previous lives.

Folami's training didn't allow her to feel such pity for long. Nor to completely comprehend the irony. For Folami was also the result of genetic tampering. Generations ago, the Olodumare Hegemony selectively altered the genes of many of its citizenry in the hopes of breeding telepaths. They were successful to a degree, as many of the descendents of those subjects, such as Folami, were able to harness their minds. As a tenth-level—the highest rating in Hegemony history—she wielded the powers of telepathy, able to read minds, and telekinesis, able to move objects with her thoughts.

She had been trained to become Ori-Inu, one of the Hegemony's cadre of telepathic agents, all memories from her life prior to training erased.

Reading fellow humans was always easy for Folami. She

understood the human thought processes by virtue of having them herself, along with a strength of perception that few, if any, shared. But the Eso were another story entirely. They had learned their lesson from the war. While the Hegemony's decisive victory had been the destruction of Yemoja, the world that served as the Oyo Empire's seat of power, it had been the Ori-Inu who had proven to be the most damaging to the Oyo during the war, using their ability to harness the mind to very good effect.

The rebels had therefore again altered the engineering of the Eso so that their thoughts barely registered as human anymore. It had taken several encounters before Folami could even go so far as to isolate their thought patterns, and even then, she couldn't make heads nor tails of *what* they were thinking. Sounds like nothing she'd ever heard, colors she didn't recognize, violent images that even her mind couldn't process properly. An occasional human thought, left over from when the Eso were properly human, poked through the horrible chaos, and indeed those had sometimes given Folami a proper point of reference.

As far as Folami knew, she was the only Ori-Inu who had mastered the trick of mindblasting the Eso to kill them. Humans, again, were not a problem—if she so desired, she could kill all the survivors of Rufiji Company with only a few seconds' concentration. But with the Eso, their thoughts were like quicksilver, difficult to get a hold of. Killing them with her mind expended effort, and she needed to ration that.

The half-dozen Eso converging on Cavalry Chief Olugbanma were almost on him, and the cavalry chief's Ayoka rifle could only go so far, surrounded as he was.

Folami ran toward him, setting up in position so the Eso were between her and Olugbanma and she set up a crossfire with her own Bayo pistol, using her telekinesis to make her aim true. The heads four of the Eso exploded in a rain of blood, bone, and brain matter.

She left only two alive, and Olugbanma was able to handle them.

"You couldn't kill the other two, save me some ammunition?" the cavalry chief asked, but Folami was already moving on. She didn't even notice the disdain or the lack of gratitude, as it was far too common among the cavalry to get worked up over.

Another Eso was bearing down on Cavalryman Olafemi, swinging one claw toward Olafemi's torso. Folami hopped onto the rebel's back. Given a choice between telekinteically halting the Eso's claw—moving against the creature's momentum—or simply getting Olafemi out of the way, she chose the latter. It expended less energy, though it did put the cavalryman in the rather undignified position of being knocked on his ass from her mental shove.

He'll thank me later, Folami thought as she gave a similar push to the Eso's claw, making its swing faster, stronger, more violent—and longer. The claw impaled the rebel in the left part of its own chest. It didn't go very far—it took a powerful strike to make it through that chitinous skin—but it was enough to open a wound.

She moved to leap off the Eso's back, but the rebel slashed at her with his other claw, the blade catching her face mask.

Yanking her head back, she managed to escape with damage only to the mask and not her person. *Now I'm* really *grateful the gas is dissipating*, she thought worriedly. As soon as she was clear, she projected right into Olafemi's mind: *Cavalryman, now!* Still on his back, Olafemi fired his Ayoka on full automatic right into the wound the Eso had given itself.

Two dozen armor-piercing rounds tore through the Eso and ripped a gash halfway across the rebel's chest.

With that opening, Folami was easily able to telekinetically grip the two ends of the wound and pry them further apart, eventually cleaving the Eso in two.

The upper part of the rebel—the part that had the brain, that was still managing to send impulses to the rest of the body— wriggled about, but the lower portion lay still.

Like all Ori-Inu, Folami wore skintight body armor. Black, with red trim, the armor protected Folami and enhanced her strength. Her telekinetic abilities could make her stronger still.

Which was good, as all that strength was required to break the claw off the dead rebel's appendage.

With a crack that would have echoed throughout Kaduna Township if the sounds of battle weren't so overwhelming, Folami did so, then took a moment to catch her breath. *Need to take it easy—there are still about seventy of the filthy* buruku *left.*

Hegemony cavalry armor was designed with strength in mind rather than agility, so Olafemi looked like a beached whale trying to clamber to his feet. With a smile, Folami took pity on him and mentally lifted him upright.

"Thanks," the cavalryman said, but his surface thoughts indicated that he resented needing the help.

Not dwelling on it, Folami moved on to fight more Eso.

She still needed her telekinesis to make the claw useful, as her own unenhanced strength was insufficient to drive the claw through the rebels' chitin, but the effort would be less than that of mindblasting.

Using a big rock as her springboard, Folami did a running leap, coming down on the back of another Eso that was about to kill Cavalry Master Apara, driving the claw through the rebel's head. Even as blood splattered everywhere, Folami yanked the claw back out, tucked into a roll, and jumped to another rebel.

The stench of the blood was starting to get to her, now that her face mask with its nasal filters had been torn.

She managed to kill another four Eso that way, but on the fourth, she drove the claw too far into the rebel's head to gain a handhold. Mentally yanking it out was an option, but before she could try, three Eso converged on her.

Reaching out, she mentally grabbed the four fresh Eso corpses, and threw them all at the three newcomers. The distraction of having to claw through the corpses of their fellow rebels was enough to allow Folami to take out her Bayo pistol and blast the rocks they were on to pieces, trapping them. She then telekinetically grabbed the claws from one and rammed them into the other two.

Surrounded for the moment only by Eso corpses, Folami cast her mind outward to the entirety of Kaduna Township. The civilians had long since been evacuated. About a quarter of the Eso who'd attacked here were dead now. Meanwhile, Rufiji Company's complement had been cut in half.

Damn it, she thought, *the mission was supposed to be over . . .*

Seven hours ago, Folami had been on the flight deck of the Hegemony Cavalry Vessel *L'owuro*, returning to Ife from a mission to Orunmila, when the distress call from Oshun had come in.

She had always enjoyed watching space on the viewer, and it was Eta-shift, an especially quiet time. That shift was the equivalent of late night, when most of the *L'owuro* crew was asleep. Only four of them were on the deck, the minimum required on the shift to ensure optimum operation.

"Amazing view, isn't it?"

Turning to her right, Folami saw one of those four people: the pilot, Cavalry Chief Adejola. Like many pilots, he'd shaved most of his head, leaving only a small, close-cropped batch of hair arranged in stylized "A" for *atuko*, or pilot.

"Yes, it's spectacular."

"I notice you only come up here when War Chief Tobi's off-shift."

Smiling, Folami said, "The war chief doesn't appreciate 'nonessentials' on the flight deck."

Adejola snorted. "Right. You're the most essential person on this ship. Rufiji Company's just here to run your code."

"Maybe, but while we're in transit, I'm just a passenger." Folami shrugged. "I don't mind—it's nice to have the downtime, especially after *that* mission. Once the war chief's back on shift, I'm going to get some sleep."

"Sounds vaguely strategic," Adejola said with a grin. "Well, I'm glad to have you up here."

Folami frowned at that, as it wasn't something she'd ever heard before. The other reason she preferred to come up here during Eta-shift was that there were fewer people. For one thing, that meant there were fewer minds to overhear. Of course, she would never pry into a person's mind without authorization, and it would take extraordinary circumstances for such authorization to ever be given on someone in the cavalry. But Folami was too strong a telepath to avoid psionic eavesdropping altogether, and she sometimes caught surface thoughts. She was issued a psi-screen, of course, but she hated using it when she was awake.

By coming onto the flight deck when it was all but empty, she got fewer looks of fear, hatred, and confusion, which were often matched by the thoughts. Flatbrains didn't like telepaths, and cavalry didn't like Ori-Inu.

Before Folami had a chance to query Adejola as to why he was glad to have her there, though, the cavalrywoman at communications spoke. "Cavalry Chief Adejola, we have an incoming distress call!"

"Source?"

The cavalrywoman put a hand to her right ear to aid in making out the sounds that were coming through the receiver hooked around her lobe. "It's Hegemony—Code 47."

Folami started. Code 47 was used by Orisha, those tasked with seeking out telepaths and making them into Ori-Inu.

Manipulating a few controls on her console, the communications officer added, "Source is Oshun. There was a refinery explosion—an unknown gas has been released into the atmosphere. The Orisha is injured, and there are indeterminate casualties from the explosion and the gas."

Adejola's primary thought was impossible for Folami to not sense: utter dread that he was going to have to wake War Chief Tobi up.

"Getting something else," the cavalrywoman added. "The Eso have claimed responsibility and are now attacking Kaduna Township."

Adejola cursed. "*Mogbe.* All right, wake the war chief up."

"With all due respect, sir," the cavalrywoman said with even more dread than Folami had sensed from Adejola, "I'd rather that you did that, as the war chief's less likely to reassign *you* to scrubbing the hull."

Adejola smiled. "Don't be so sure that he wouldn't, Cavalrywoman. But yeah, I'll do it."

An excessively cranky War Chief Tobi stumbled onto the

flight deck minutes later. He was wearing a hastily thrown-on dashiki, and nothing else. Folami had only seen the war chief in full uniform, and his excessively hairy, bony legs were something of a surprise. After all, atop his head, he had close-cropped, thinning white hair. Like many men of status in the Hegemony, he had taken to wearing a thick beard, akin to that of Oba Isembi, which was the same white as what little hair he had.

Even in his nightclothes, though, he had a Bayo pistol strapped to a shoulder holster.

Loudly, Adejola said, "War chief on deck!"

Much more loudly, Tobi declared: "Cavalry Chief, you have seven-and-a-half seconds to explain why you awakened me from a wonderful dream about the spectacular sex I was having with your mother." His words echoed off the unstaffed consoles.

Swallowing, Adejola quickly filled the war chief in. Folami couldn't help but smile at the image that came into Adejola's head, which was of Tobi in bed with his mother, no matter how hard the pilot tried to banish it.

"It's a lucky thing for you this was serious," Tobi said as he fell more than sat into the command chair. Technically, regulations were that whoever was in command of the flight deck sat there, but everyone on *L'owuro* learned quickly that only the war chief's ass was allowed to touch the seat. "Change course to Oshun, Cavalry Chief."

"Changing course," Adejola said smartly.

Tobi turned to his left. "Any other ships in the area?"

The cavalryman at tactical—who had never actually been in the same room with the war chief before, and Folami felt his disappointment in the reality after hearing the reputation, though she suspected the hairy, bony legs had a lot to do with that—said, "No military ships, sir, no."

"Cavalryman, do you *honestly* think I care about non-military ships?"

Suddenly, the tac officer was less disappointed and more scared. "Uh, no, sir, I don't suppose you—"

"That sentence ends at 'no, sir,' Cavalryman, unless you want to be scrubbing the hull for the next month."

"Yes, sir," he said quickly.

"Cavalry Chief Adejola, ETA to Oshun?"

"Seven hours, sir."

Then, for the first time, Tobi acknowledged Folami's presence. "What're *you* doing up here, Ori-Inu?"

"Admiring the view," Folami said simply.

Misconstruing, Tobi was suddenly self-conscious of his state of undress. Rising to his feet, he said, "Cavalry Chief Adejola, you have the deck."

"I acknowledge command of the deck, sir," Adejola said formally, which was more for the benefit of the flight recorder than the war chief.

Even before *L'owuro* made orbit of Oshun, Folami had felt the strange images and unknowable instincts of the Eso in her mind. The tac officer reported that the gas from the refinery explosion was dispersing, but he was unable to identify what the gas *was*. Given that *L'owuro*, like all military ships, had an extensive catalogue of every gas known to humanity—mainly so that the personnel on board knew how to defend themselves against it—this was unusual.

Tobi summoned Rufiji Company to the dropship bay. The cavalry all came in, not quite at double-time—that wasn't really possible in the bulky armor—but they lumbered in single-file through the metal corridors of *L'owuro*, dozens of armored boots clanging on the deck to create a cacophony that only multiple missions had inured Folami to. The deafening report of metal on metal was just background noise to her now, though when she first started performing missions for the Hegemony, the sound had threatened to drive her mad.

In the bay itself, dozens of dropships were lined up to be disgorged through the *L'owuro*'s belly and into Oshun's atmosphere. Each drop held eight armored personnel, and Tobi watched as each one was filled and deployed. For whatever reason, Tobi always preferred to go down on the final ship, leaving Rufiji's direct commander, Cavalry Master Fasina, to take the first drop down.

As usual, Folami joined Tobi in the final drop to disembark. Other cavalry commanders had wanted the Ori-Inu to be on the first drop, but Tobi felt it was best to, as he put it, "save the best for last." Folami had never understood this philosophy, but it was important enough to Tobi—and she was sufficiently uninterested in engaging him in an argument on the subject— that she simply went along with it.

Also as usual, Tobi didn't say a word to her, indeed barely acknowledged her existence, for the entire drop.

As the dropship plummeted through Oshun's atmosphere, rocking back and forth in the turbulence of air currents, Folami tuned out her immediate surroundings and focused her mind on the surface below.

She felt very few human minds anywhere near the Eso, beyond those of Rufiji Company. This relieved Folami, as it meant that local authorities had evacuated the population of Kaduna Township after the explosion. With luck, this would mean there would be a comparatively small body count when the dropships hit dirt. Eso attacks were almost always accompanied by appalling civilian casualties.

The final drop landed with a soft thud, thrusters decelerating the drop enough to make for a smooth landing on the muddy ground.

Even as Folami prepared to disembark, she sensed Cavalry Master Fasina stuffing a grenade down a rebel's throat—and then a moment later, the cavalry master's agonized pain as the chitin of the exploding Eso tore through his armor, rending his left arm from its shoulder.

Exiting the drop, she saw that a group of nearby rebels were wounded enough by their exploding comrade that they were vulnerable to Ayoka fire from Cavalry Master Morayo and a dozen of her troops.

The place they had landed was a park located next to the refinery that had exploded. Northwest of their location was a giant maze of twisted metal, still smoking from the explosion that had started this whole thing. Right in front of her, dozens of Eso swarmed about the mud and grass and scorched earth, like maggots crawling over a giant, pockmarked corpse.

From there, the battle was joined, with Folami doing her part, killing several Eso, albeit at the cost of damage to her face mask.

Folami felt as if a spike were being driven through her left eye from her repeated psionic exertions. Even she, at the tenth level, had her limits, and with this mission so soon after dealing with those terrorists on Orunmila, she wasn't sure how much more she could handle.

But handle it, she would. This was what she was trained for.

They had been on Orunmila for a week, taking care of those separatists in their fortified base. Unlike the Eso, who wanted to bring back the glory days of the Oyo Empire, these were religious fanatics who just wanted to be out of the Hegemony. It hadn't been a particularly difficult assignment, but it was a long one, and normally after so grueling a mission, Folami would have been allocated some time to rest.

I haven't been this tired since Nupe.

The thought made her look quickly around. Her first instinct was that she'd accidentally read someone else's mind, which sometimes happened when she was fatigued. The only place named Nupe she knew of was on Yemoja before it was destroyed. As far as she remembered, she'd never been there.

But no, the thought was her own.

Before she could try to examine this, she saw ten Eso converging on three cavalry who were standing back-to-back-to-back in a circle near the remains of a running path. Surrounded by Eso and unable to move, the trio kept throwing Ayoka rounds that ricocheted off the rebels.

The Eso's greatest vulnerability was the same one that most living creatures had: their eyes. Unfortunately, they were almost impossible to hit in general, and the Oyo rebels had bred the Eso with eyes that were small and covered on both sides by folds of chitinous flesh.

The only way to hit them was to be the system's most perfect shot.

With her telekinesis, Folami was just that.

She fired twenty shots at the eyes of the ten Eso.

The headache was making her ears ring now. She couldn't even make out what it was one of the cavalry was saying to her.

No way I can do that trick again.

Including War Chief Tobi, Rufiji Company had fifty-nine people assigned to it, and now thirty-four of them were dead.

By the time Folami could mindblast each of the fifty-plus Eso left, Rufiji would be wiped out, and Folami herself might not make it that far alive.

Calling down a strike from *L'owuro* wasn't an option, as this was a populated area, they hadn't found the Orisha who sent the distress call yet, and all the evidence of the explosion and the strange gas would be lost, so no one would ever know what happened here. Her duty to the Hegemony was to make sure that this could be investigated properly.

So the orbital strike was only a final option, and she wasn't there yet. According to what the flight deck had said before the drops were launched, reinforcements wouldn't arrive for another day.

Maybe I can fry all their brains at once, like I did those people in Nupe.

Again, Folami startled herself. That thought also came out of nowhere, and was most definitely her own, not someone else's. *What is going on?*

That thought was cut short by the realization that an Eso claw was coming down toward her head. She dove to the ground, then shot her Bayo at the mud the rebel was running through, which came nowhere near the Eso.

Get it together, she chastised herself, as she re-aimed, the rounds this time crashing into the Eso's hard shell.

That got him to turn toward her. Folami gazed into his eyes and then fried his brain.

For whatever reason, though, she knew—just *knew*—that once, in the past, she had fried the brains of two dozen people at once. As a tenth-level, that was completely possible, but it wasn't anything she'd even considered trying, nor even been in a position to try.

But the Eso were wearing Rufiji down. She had to make the attempt.

She broadcast her thoughts: *War Chief Tobi, clear out. I can stop the rest of the Eso, but I can't do it with Rufiji Company underfoot. Get to the drops and get back to L'owuro.*

Tobi's voice sounded in Folami's earpiece, a method of communication far less secure. "Back to the drops? We can't—"

War Chief, if you don't do this, the rest of Rufiji will die. Sound the retreat!

Reluctantly, Tobi gave the order. Four cavalry lay down covering fire while the rest of the survivors of Rufiji retreated to the dropships.

Only one tree was still standing in the park, a thick, gnarled oak. Folami ran toward it after the drops took off, shooting her Bayo indiscriminately behind her to keep the Eso still chasing her at a distance. Nimbly, she climbed up as high as she could, the high ground giving her precious moments to collect herself. The rebels would be able to climb up after her, but soon, that wouldn't be an issue.

Because either her plan would work, or she'd be dead.

She took three deep breaths through her nose, exhaling through her mouth.

Two Eso started clambering up the twisted trunk of the oak, heading right for her.

She let out the most primal of screams.

"She's waking up!"

Folami blinked the bright spots out of her eyes at the voice of the Rufiji medic, Doctor Modupe. Sitting upright quickly proved to be a mistake, as the universe spun around in ever-faster circles. She had an odd feeling on her upper lip, and put a gloved hand there.

Dried blood chipped off.

Lying slowly back down, she realized that she was on the ground under the oak tree. Modupe was kneeling over her, checking his diagnostic scanner.

"What happened?" she asked.

Modupe scratched his stubbly chin. The young doctor had neglected to shave in an attempt to make himself look older. He looked like he had a ravaged forest on his baby face. "You tell us. The war chief came back to *L'owuro,* and the flight deck reported that the Eso were all dead. He came back, dragged my ass away from my patients to come down with him, only to find you unconscious and a whole lotta dead rebels."

"Will she live?" That was Tobi, who had approached.

"Probably. Can I get back to *L'owuro* now? I've got a dozen wounded up there, and—"

"Permission granted," Tobi said, and Folami could feel his irritation at the doctor's whining.

Reaching into a case, Modupe took out a small plastic bottle and offered it to Folami. "Here—take these for the pain." Then he got to his feet and wandered off.

Tobi glared down at her through his beard. "Neat trick you pulled, Ori-Inu. Didn't think even you could wipe that many in one shot."

She sat up more slowly this time. "I didn't, either. And I'm in no rush to do it again."

"You shouldn't have to. Oh, and we found who summoned us here."

Clambering gingerly to her feet, Folami followed Tobi, who led her to the dropship, which had a medical pallet being loaded onto it. The occupant wore the loose-fitting white robes of an Orisha. His round face was scarred by burns.

"His ID says his name is—" Tobi started, but Folami interrupted.

"Hembadoon."

Tobi scowled at her. "Yeah, well, we didn't have you around to read him, but—"

But Folami interrupted him a second time. "You don't understand, War Chief—I can barely read surface thoughts in the shape I'm in, and right now, this man's too far gone to *have* surface thoughts. No, I *know* him."

"From where?"

She shook her head. "I have no idea."

TWO
Ife — four days ago

HEMBADOON LOVED MEETING WITH OBA Isembi. Not because he had any great love for the man. Quite the opposite, in fact, and Hembadoon knew the feeling was mutual. Isembi viewed Hembadoon with contempt and disdain. One of the advantages Isembi had, being Oba of the Hegemony, supreme ruler of all the worlds in the system, destroyer of Yemoja, was that if he didn't like someone, he simply could get rid of them.

But the disadvantage was that he would have to accept the consequences.

The day Hembadoon lived in fear of was the day that Isembi or one of his minions found an Orisha who could do the job as well as Hembadoon. He knew that day was coming. It was inevitable—there was simply no way that he could be the best forever.

However, Hembadoon had every intention of delaying that day as long as possible by continuing to seek out and train the finest Ori-Inu he could. As long as he did so, Isembi could do nothing to Hembadoon.

The room where they had their meeting was in Isembi's imperial palace in Benin, the capital city on Ife, the homeworld. The three-story structure was circular, as was proper, with

Isembi's throne room on the ground floor, where he would meet publicly with applicants. On the upper floor was his bedchamber, where he would rest after each day's work as the leader of the greatest empire the universe had ever known.

On the middle floor was the private meeting room where most of the Hegemony's business truly got done. The walls appeared to be made of adobe, but Hembadoon knew that was an illusion to put people at ease that they were in as ordinary a place as a palace could be. In truth, the walls were reinforced to withstand an orbital bombardment. A tapestry hung on one section of the wall, a crescent-shaped wooden table against another section, and a burning fire in the center that made the entire room smell like smoked cedar. That last was a silly extravagance, even in a building filled with them, as it was midsummer in Benin, and the room was perfectly temperature controlled in any case.

But it made the room look and smell elegant. For Isembi, appearances were of tremendous importance.

Isembi was standing at a sideboard near the desk while chatting with a holographic image projected over the firepit. He wore the traditional red robes of an Oba going back as far as anyone could remember. His wild white hair was restrained by a ponytail, and his beard remained thick. Hembadoon knew that many men of the Hegemony had styled their hair or worn beards in that style—or both—out of respect for the Oba.

Which was why Hembadoon kept his own head and cheeks shaved clean.

Though they were the same height, Hembadoon always felt shorter than Isembi. The Oba carried himself as if he were the tallest person in the room. He practically oozed charisma. *Which*, Hembadoon often thought wryly, *is the only reason why this snake in the grass has become Oba.*

Isembi was holding a thick-bottomed glass with a clear liquid. He was speaking to the holographic image, which was of a face covered in what looked like orange fur. Hembadoon knew that this was one of the Hegemony's trading partners from beyond the system, though he couldn't recall what the people were called. He rarely concerned himself with external matters.

"Would you mind explaining where your shipment is, Horrr?" Isembi asked testily.

"Sorry I am, Oba," Horrr said, "but gone is the shipment. Hit we were by the *Dread Remora*—"

Holding up a hand, Isembi said, "I don't wish to hear excuses, Horrr, I wish to receive the merchandise I paid for."

"Get it you will. Restock on Frrren's Landing we shall and come back we will within two weeks—return on the first Ishegun of Erele."

Hembadoon was impressed that this Horrr person had gone to the trouble of learning the Hegemony calendar. Then again, one thing the Orisha did know was that this system was plentiful in metals that were of great value outside the Hegemony, so it behooved Horrr as a regular trader to be familiar.

"The shipment will be half again as large, yes?"

Horrr winced. "Not the terms to which we—"

"We agreed that the shipment would already be here, and you've already received our iron and platinum. I believe the delay of two weeks justifies a fifty percent increase in the value of our goods, yes? If not, I am perfectly happy to find someone *else* to take our—"

Speaking quickly, Horrr said, "Necessary that will not be, Oba. As you say is as it will."

"Excellent." Isembi provided an insincere smile, then touched a control on one of his many earrings. The holographic image winked out.

Turning to the Orisha, Isembi's smile remained unchanged. "Welcome back, Hembadoon."

Pointing at the firepit, Hembadoon asked, "Don't you have people to handle such mundane matters?"

"When they go smoothly, yes. However, Horrr was being difficult and I felt the need to step in. Especially since I doubt he was truly raided by pirates, he probably simply found another buyer." He shook his head. "If I believed every story I've heard about the so-called *Dread Remora*, the ship would have to be in twelve places simultaneously—and I honestly don't believe that the vessel truly exists." Letting out a breath, he held up his glass. "May I offer you a drink? It's from Esu."

"Really?" Hembadoon moved to sit at the guest chair next to the desk. His feet hurt after standing completely still through six different security checkpoints before being allowed to set foot in the palace. At that, he was fortunate—were he not an Orisha, he would have had to go through fifteen. "I was unaware that there *were* any drinks from Esu." The once-frozen world on the outskirts of the system had only a small, fledgling colony that was slowly performing terraforming tasks. The long-term goal was to make the place as habitable as Ife, but in the short term, life was very hard on the still-mostly-frozen planet.

As Isembi poured the liquid into another glass, he said, "So few things grow in the ground on Esu. But an enterprising young couple thought they would be able to produce alcohol. This is from their first bottle of what they claim to be gin, which they generously gave to me as a gift. We're hoping they'll be able to do business similar to the distilleries on Oshun and Oya."

Hembadoon took the glass from Isembi, who then sat down at the desk, perpendicular to where the Orisha had sat down. The drink had a sharp odor, cutting through his nostrils and wiping out the cedary smell of the fire. Taking a small sip, Hembadoon felt the alcohol burn in his throat so fiercely that it masked whatever taste the gin might have had. A good drink created a warm glow in the base of the neck, but this was *not* a good drink. After letting out a gasp, Hembadoon said, "I hope you aren't relying upon this elixir to spur Esu's economy."

Isembi smiled. "Hardly. And this *is* the first bottle. It is part of our *long-term* plan to accelerate Esu's schedule."

Hembadoon nodded, setting the glass down with a clunk on the wooden table.

"The report I read," Isembi was saying, "said that you found a new telepath in the hinterlands of Oya."

Snorting, Hembadoon said, "'Hinterlands' is the polite word for it, yes. These were hill people, living deep in the valleys of the Jukun Mountains. The most recent technology they possessed was a century old, and most had no idea of how to use it. Oh, and they are *fiercely* protective of their own, so the notion of a stranger in white robes taking one of them away from home sat very poorly with them."

"But you managed."

"Barely—I almost died." Hembadoon smiled. "Sorry to disappoint you."

"And lose such a valuable resource? Don't be ridiculous. You see, Hembadoon, of all the Hegemony's many government assets, by far the most vital are the Ori-Inu. The threats we face are so great, that our best line of defense are these telepaths. That makes a good Orisha of great value." The Oba leaned forward. "You, Hembadoon, are a *very* good Orisha." Then he leaned back and sighed. "Would that the same could be said of your colleagues. The fact is, the skill set required to perform your task is difficult to find in a single person. You are one of the few."

Raising his glass in acknowledgment of this rare compliment, Hembadoon decided not to actually drink anymore of the Esu concoction.

Isembi stood up and moved toward the firepit, his back to the Orisha. "It is because of your unique skills that I require you for your next mission. I wish you to go to Oshun." He turned around to face him once again, and Hembadoon saw that Isembi looked almost angry. Emotions rarely made it to the Oba's face, so he was obviously quite displeased indeed. "Another Ori-Inu has disappeared."

Hembadoon blinked. "An Ori-Inu has disappeared?" Then he shook his head. "Wait—*another* Ori-Inu has disappeared? How many?"

"This is the sixth, and we're fairly certain they've been taken. Their neural implants have been either blocked or removed and destroyed."

Angrily, Hembadoon stood up. "Why was I never informed of this?"

Unmoved by his anger, Isembi shrugged. "The information was classified."

"Nothing involving the Ori-Inu should be classified from *any* Orisha—least of all from *me!*"

Now Isembi fixed Hembadoon with a cold, hard glare. "I am Oba, Hembadoon. I decide what should or should not be. Not you."

"Who has gone missing?"

"The latest is Abeje. The others include Akanke, Baderinwa,

Ige, Olufunke, and Taiwo."

Hembadoon shook his head. He had found and trained half of those, including Abeje. In fact, she was his third-best student.

Second-best if you only counted the ones who made it through to the end.

"If it was *so* important that this be kept from me before, why are you telling me *now*?"

Reaching into one of the pockets in his robes, Isembi took out a reader and tossed it onto the desk. "These are the reports of the disappearances, including investigations made by other Ori-Inu. Only the last one isn't there—from Abeje. She was on a mission to assassinate an Oyo spy when the signal from her implant went out."

"On Oshun?"

Isembi nodded. "Though she doesn't recall this, of course, Abeje is from Oshun. We were hoping that might have aided in the search for this spy, but that approach obviously was flawed. I am now assigning this to you. For the duration of this mission, Hembadoon, your clearance has been raised to seventh level."

That got Hembadoon to raise an eyebrow. Orisha normally only had fifth-level clearance.

Isembi continued. "Among other things, this means that you may download the contents of that reader to your robe's computer."

Nodding, Hembadoon sat down at the desk and subvocalized instructions to the computer woven into the fabric of his white robe to do that very thing.

Walking back to the desk, Isembi set down his glass, and then rested his palms on the surface, leaning in toward Hembadoon, close enough that the Orisha could smell the mediocre gin on the Oba's breath. "You leave first thing in the morning. Understand, Orisha, I want my Ori-Inu back very much. Go find them."

That got Hembadoon's attention. Just as Hembadoon refused to refer to Isembi by his title, the Oba never referred to Hembadoon as "Orisha," as was proper.

That he did so now bespoke the urgency of the situation. Dryly, he said, "Yes, *sir*," then gulped down the rest of his gin. The burn was a bit less this time—though it was as likely as not that the first sip anaesthetized his mouth—and almost approached the possibility of having a taste. Hembadoon let out a noise that sounded vaguely like the moan of an animal caught in a trap, and moved to the exit.

"You risk much, Hembadoon," Isembi said as the door slid aside at the Orisha's approach.

Hembadoon stopped short. "I'm not risking a damn thing. You can't afford to kill me. Nobody has found as many Ori-Inu as I, nobody has trained as many as I. And I know what you have carefully kept from the history texts. Everyone assumes that the Cavalry destroyed Yemoja and won the war. But it was the Ori-Inu—*my* Ori-Inu—who did the true work of bringing the Oyo down. You owe me your throne, mighty Oba, and that debt continues to accrue with every passing day. The day you kill me is three days before you lose the throne you worked so hard to acquire, little as I relish the prospect. We keep each other nicely in our respective places." Hembadoon grinned. "I have nothing to lose, so I might as well enjoy it."

With that, he departed for his mission.

As an Orisha, Hembadoon was assigned a small, one-person craft—though a passenger could cram in behind the flight chair in a pinch—that he'd named the *Ebun*. The ship had a magnificent sound system and a huge library of music, at his insistence. If he had to travel all by himself for days on end, he at least wanted something to listen to.

For the trip to Oshun, which was three days from Ife at *Ebun*'s top speed, he found himself gravitating toward Yetinde spirituals. Hembadoon was a devout agnostic, and believed in pretty much no gods or demiurges or creators or anything like that, but *damn* the religious types from Yetinde could put a tune together. One group in particular, which called itself Sunshine on Days of Rain, had amazing harmonies that sounded particularly compelling in the state-of-the-art system he had in *Ebun*, and the power of their talking drums vibrated in the base of his spine.

It also helped Hembadoon deal with his space sickness. While his robes dealt with the actual nausea by delivering medication directly into his bloodstream, his anxiety regarding the possibility of getting sick required music as a coping mechanism.

One thing that wouldn't ameliorate his space sickness—but would at least distract him—was the first interview he had to conduct in his investigation. Often, when Ori-Inu went into the field, they went with a cavalry unit as backup and support. For her trip to Oshun, Abeje was supported by Sankarani Company.

Hembadoon had little patience for the cavalry, mostly because they had been resistant to the notion of Ori-Inu being attached to their units. Never mind the fact that the presence of an Ori-Inu increased the likelihood of the unit making it through their engagement with minimal casualties.

He supposed that they resented being responsible for someone not part of their chain of command, but Hembadoon had always been more interested in results than process.

When he put the call through to Sankarani, he used the priority frequency for Orisha, which required that the commanding officer answer it. Anyone else responding to that frequency was a court-martial offense, both for the CO who didn't reply to it and for the poor fool who did.

So it was the ever-scowling mahogany-skinned face of War Chief Titilayo that looked back at him from the holographic projector on his console.

"Orisha Hembadoon. You're still alive."

"War Chief Titilayo. I could say the same."

She smiled. "Psychopaths do well in Oba Isembi's cavalry, hadn't you heard?"

Hembadoon snorted. "You're not a psychopath. Psychopaths don't know they're psychopaths. You're a high-functioning sociopath."

"And you're not a psychiatrist, so how would you know?"

He waved a hand. "Fine, you're a psychopath."

"What does an Orisha need with this particular psychopath?"

"I need to ask you about your mission to Oshun."

The smile dropped. "We were to escort the Ori-Inu to the planet," Titilayo said tightly, "and provide support as needed."

Easy enough for Hembadoon to read between the lines: Titilayo didn't know the specifics of Abeje's mission. That wasn't a surprise, as Isembi preferred to get rid of spies as quietly as possible without the public even knowing they existed.

Of course, that also meant that the Oyo spy was probably still on Oshun somewhere.

"Did she ever ask for that support?"

"No. And then she went missing. Our last tag on her was in a refinery in Kaduna Township. After that, nothing. We did a full-target search, but she wasn't anywhere on Oshun. So we reported in and got reassigned. Honestly, I thought we were done with that."

For a brief instant, Hembadoon toyed with the notion that Titilayo was the one responsible for the disappearance, but that didn't track. Psychopath or sociopath, she had always been loyal to the Hegemony.

After signing off with the war chief, he put the music back on. It was an *a cappella* number by Sunshine on Days of Rain, and the power of their harmonies echoed off *Ebun*'s bulkhead.

The next step was to do a computer dive, to cross reference the various Ori-Inu disappearance reports, searching for any common terms. The search turned up nothing that gave him any encouragement: "mysterious," "confused," "unsure." The words "planet" and "station" appeared fairly often, and specific places turned up a lot, particularly Ife, Benin, Niger (the city that housed the Ori-Inu training facility), and Olokun.

Of all the results of the search, "Olokun" was the only one that wasn't in any way familiar. Hembadoon frowned. One of the first things he learned in his own training as an Orisha was that the discrepant part of a set was the one that usually was of the most interest.

The music program moved on to a hard-driving number that always set Hembadoon's pulse pounding in much the same way a good investigation did, and he found himself amused by the serendipity of it starting right when he started to check out "Olokun." Uses of the term in the reports consisted of either a word overheard by witnesses or a reference to an Olokun Station. Hembadoon searched the computer for other uses of the term, but the only hits that generated were mythical ones relating to the founding of the cradle of life on Ife. Ironically, one of the religious hits was to the lyrics for one of the Sunshine on Days of Rain songs he'd been listening to an hour ago.

So what is Olokun Station? There was no record of any station with that designation—and thanks to his new seventh-level clearance, Hembadoon had access to a whole new range of classified files he wouldn't have been able to get at in the past.

But there was nothing, aside from a few mentions in these reports and the myths.

The question continued to nag at Hembadoon until he reached Oshun. The first thing he did was contact the planet's orbital control, which was located in Kaduna Station in high orbit. The Kaduna Mining Corporate all but owned Oshun. The planet's two main cities were Kaduna Township and Kaduna City, and it was difficult to find anything on that world that didn't have the company name in evidence.

"Kaduna Station, this is Orisha Hembadoon aboard the *Ebun*." He sent that on the same priority frequency he used to contact Titilayo.

A friendly female voice replied a few seconds later. "Kaduna Station responding. Welcome to Oshun, Orisha Hembadoon. What can we do for you today?"

Well, I thought I'd lift my robes and ask you to fellate me in the town square. Somehow, Hembadoon managed to restrain himself from saying that, especially since he suspected that the woman on the other end would do so rather than risk the ire of the Oba's favorite government agency. Instead, he simply said, "I need a landing point in Kaduna Township, preferably close to the refinery."

"Not a problem, Orisha. We're uploading a landing vector for *Ebun* right now."

Almost instantly, that vector showed up on *Ebun*'s heads-up display. "Thank you very kindly, Kaduna Station."

"If there's anything you need from the people of Oshun, please don't hesitate to ask. If you contact the Municipal Building in Kaduna Township, there's someone there twenty-one hours a day."

"Good to know. Thanks for your help. *Ebun* out."

The refinery was, Hembadoon thought, a testament to the hideousness of industry.

He supposed it was inevitable. After all, nobody built a refinery with aesthetics in mind. Form didn't just follow function when you were refining ores and minerals and things, it pretty much dogged its every step. Ugly metal passageways connected ugly metal structures to other ugly metal structures, with ports that released heat into the air.

Proving that the owners weren't entirely without a sense of humor, there was a verdant, beautiful park right next to it. Hembadoon figured it was an attempt to beautify the area, but the park was maybe a quarter the size of the refinery. All its grassy, tree-lined presence served to do was shine a light on just how ass-ugly the refinery was.

Inside was little better, all metal walls and floors with no decoration. The executives who ran the refinery were in a different location. What few offices there were on-site belonged to lower-management functionaries who were obviously too busy making their quotas to even go so far as to decorate their working space.

It didn't take long for Hembadoon to find the right person to talk to about Abeje. Nobody knew anything about an Ori-Inu being present at the refinery—so it was obvious that her investigation was a covert one, which tracked with the mission profile—but each person he spoke to mentioned one of the engineers, a man named Kosoko, going completely insane.

His last stop was yet another lower-management functionary: an officious twit of a personnel manager. Hembadoon sat in his office while the short, balding man explained in a squeaky, sing-songy voice from behind his clean metal desk that Kosoko was perfectly normal until a few days ago.

"It was *incredibly* strange. One day he was working with the others, and making his usual *awful* puns, and then suddenly he was babbling like an idiot and banging his *head* against the wall."

Hembadoon frowned. "Are you being metaphorical, or—?"

The manager made a *tch* noise. "No, he *really* was hitting his head against the wall. They had to take him to the *police station*."

Subvocalizing instructions to his robe computer to provide directions from here to the nearest law-enforcement headquarters, Hembadoon asked, "Was he charged?"

"No, no, it was just for his *protection*—and *ours*, to be honest. I think he was going to *kill* poor Iyapo. She's the one he shared his office with. I *swear* he was raving like an Eso on crink."

Somehow, Hembadoon didn't think a drugged-out Eso would act anything like how Kosoko was behaving, but he didn't care enough to correct the man's misapprehension. He just said, "Thanks for your help."

As he exited the office, his robe computer provided the location of the Kaduna Police Headquarters. It was just a hundred meters from the refinery, which was an easy walk across the park. As he ambled over, he checked the police records, to find that Kosoko had been taken into custody on the same day that Abeje had disappeared.

While the refinery was all cold metal and fancy machinery, police HQ was a drab prefabricated structure. The officer at the desk—a polite young woman—escorted him to the cell where Kosoko was being held. She led him down a flight of unevenly spaced stairs that creaked with each step.

Widening his eyes to try to make things out in the dim light of the basement, Hembadoon saw several holding cells with the standard shockbars keeping the prisoners in their place. Each cell had a refresher, though none of them looked as though they'd been cleaned in years, and there were no windows. Only four cells were occupied. A couple of them made half-hearted cat-calls at the officer, which she ignored.

Kosoko was a short man, mid-twenties, with kinky red hair kept long on the sides and completely shaved on top—a fairly common style on Oshun among younger folks. The hair was dirty and greasy, but Hembadoon figured he hadn't been offered much by way of hygiene care since being placed in here. He was seated on the edge of the metal bunk, hugging himself with skinny arms, and rocking back and forth.

"Out of nowhere just out of nowhere people just appearing like nothing and yelling and screaming and fighting . . ."

Hembadoon set his robe computer to scan Kosoko and also record everything he said, then turned to the officer. "He been like this the whole time?"

She nodded. "When he got here, he was a lot more—well, intense. And active. Some doctors examined him, and one gave him pills to calm him, but no one's been able to get through to him."

Turning back to the cell, Hembadoon asked, "Kosoko, can you hear me?"

"Just out of nowhere couldn't believe it just the two of them going to Olokun and then coming out of nowhere . . ."

Olokun again. If there was any doubt in Hembadoon's mind

that Kosoko's sudden madness was connected to Abeje, it was gone now. "Kosoko, can you tell me about the two people? You said they were going to—"

"Out of nowhere just showing up like that and fighting and killing and yelling and screaming and who's who and I didn't know what to do with no orders . . ."

"What orders, Kosoko?" Hembadoon asked. "Whose orders were you waiting for?"

"Just completely out of nowhere . . ."

"*Mogbe,*" he muttered. Kosoko was an engineer who built equipment for the refinery to use. He had no military record, so it was unlikely that he would think in terms of "orders."

Unless he's the one Abeje came here to assassinate.

"Going to kill me going to kill each other going to kill everyone all going to die die die die die . . ." Kosoko started rocking back and forth more quickly.

"Kosoko, look at me, please. My name's Hembadoon, I'm an Orisha. I need to know—"

"Need to know, need to know, we all need to know, need to know when to go ahead, need to know when to go forward, need to know when to get a move on, need to know need to know need to know . . ."

The officer looked helplessly at Hembadoon. "See what I mean? Best psychiatrists on Oshun couldn't get through, so you probably aren't going to, either."

"I don't need to get through to him, I just need to get information out of him." Hembadoon didn't add that he'd already gotten some.

But he needed more. *If only—*

Suddenly, his computer sent him an alarm. The scan detected a low-frequency connection between a microscopic regulator implanted in Kosoko's heart—which was in his medical records as something to settle an arrhythmia—and something in the refinery.

"*Mogbe*," Hembadoon muttered, then subvocalized an instruction to the computer to have *Ebun* do a scan of the refinery, focusing on the other end of that connection.

"Won't take me, won't take me, won't take me! You can't! I'll kill everything before I let you take me away, you *buruku*!"

Whirling around, Hembadoon saw that Kosoko had risen from the bed. His bloodshot eyes were now wide, and his mouth was wide open and screaming.

"I won't go! I'll do my job you'll see you stupid *buruku* you won't take me to Olokun or anywhere else!"

The officer had her Bayo pistol out. "Sit down, Kosoko."

But Kosoko kept advancing on the shockbars. "You can't make me even if you come out of nowhere I'm still gonna do it, you hear, I'm gonna do it!"

Kosoko grabbed the bars, then screamed much louder, this time in pain, as electricity shot through his arms and body.

He fell to the floor. The officer continued to point her Bayo at him. "That's right," she said, "now get up and sit back on the bunk."

But Hembadoon noticed that Kosoko was now grabbing his chest with his left hand, his face contorted into a rictus of pain, his right hand extended stiffly. "He's having a heart attack!"

While the officer called for medical help, Hembadoon had his robe computer scan Kosoko again. The current from the shockbars had caused the regulator to burn out. *The stress of that plus going mad probably put him in defibrilation*, Hembadoon thought.

Just then, *Ebun*'s computer informed him that there was a

seventy-five percent possibility that the device in the refinery that was connected to the regulator was a disguised explosive.

Hembadoon felt the blood drain from his face as he quickly put it all together. *A dead man's switch. If he dies . . .*

Even as the Orisha thought it, Kosoko fell face first on the floor, unmoving.

The explosion happened only a second later.

THREE
An unnamed ship

YOU'RE FIVE, AND YOU WATCH as the governess is sent away. You told Daddy that she said something mean. The governess swears up and down that she never would say such a thing, but you heard it loud and clear.

You're sixteen, and a new recruit joins training. His mother is Oba Isembi's cousin. You waste little time in correcting his misapprehension that his mother's being related to the Oba makes him in any way desirable.

You're six, and your parents realize that one of your tutors is going to have to be a telepath in order to help you get your psionic abilities under control.

You're eleven, with puberty blossoming, and you know what every single boy who stares at you is thinking. You're torn between revulsion and fascination.

You're fifteen, and your first training exercise is a complete disaster. You've never been so scared in your life.

You're four, and you don't know why it hurts so very, very much when your cat dies, why you didn't just see him die, but you felt him die and it was just the worst feeling in the universe . . .

You're nineteen, and you go on your first mission as an Ori-Inu, weapons fire blasting all around you, and you master the fear with ease.

You're twenty, and a shadowy figure comes at you from behind a processor at the refinery on Oshun, and suddenly it hurts in your mind even worse than when the cat died . . .

Abeje woke up screaming.

The images from her nightmares started to fade. She tried to mentally grab them, to recall what they were, but they were like quicksilver, slipping away.

Those were memories. Those were my memories!

She couldn't maintain a grasp on them, or on anything else. Even though she should have been wide awake—every time she awoke from a nightmare that she could recall, she was instantly alert, until now—her mind was still foggy.

Fighting through the haze that covered her thoughts like a rough blanket, she endeavored to take in her surroundings.

I'm lying down, I'm out of my armor. I had a governess? No, no, focus, worry about that later. Why am I out of my armor?

The simple act of propping herself up on her elbows required a tremendous effort. The room was dark. Unable to see a thing with her eyes, she reached out psionically, which was, oddly, less of a struggle than sitting up had been.

There were no other minds in the immediate vicinity. She wasn't sure if that was a good thing or not.

Alone and naked in the dark.

The latter was an exaggeration—she appeared to be in a gown of some kind—but without her armor and her Bayo pistol, she might as well have been naked. Abeje didn't feel complete without a HUD, instant access to a computer, and the weight of her rifle in her hands or on her holster.

I'm actually from Oshun?

Need to focus.

Two sensations were wrong. She wasn't sure what they were, though.

Mogbe, woman, focus!

One was a small puncture in her right arm. It didn't actually hurt, but it felt odd. The other was an odd feeling in her shoulder—like something was pulling on her skin at the clavicle.

Why can't I remember what happened? she wondered as she felt her right arm with her left.

It wasn't just a puncture. There was an IV attached.

Without a second thought, she yanked the tube out. Pain cut through her forearm as the IV ripped through flesh.

Shouldn't have done that. It hurt. No, it's okay. Pain is good. Besides, whatever they're pumping into me can't be good.

I had a cat?

Next she felt her left shoulder with her fingers, only to find a sliver of plastic skin. Abeje knew the sensation of the artificial dermis well, from her many times being injured in the field. *Was I hit in the shoulder?*

The gown over the shoulder was wet and sticky with what Abeje realized had to be her own blood.

Then she remembered what was in that spot on her shoulder.

The neural implant. You have got *to be kidding me.*

Abeje's thoughts started to get ever-more-slowly coherent. Whatever was in that IV was apparently what kept her disoriented.

Her eyes were also adjusting to the darkness. Now she could make out shapes: long, round cylinders against the walls; small metal tables near the pallet on which she lay.

Again, she reached out with her mind. Again, she sensed nothing. But it was easier this time.

Inhaling slowly through her nose, and exhaling through her mouth, Abeje finally managed to achieve focus.

I was on Oshun. I was talking with that engineer, Kosoko.

Then what?

Closing her eyes, she concentrated, tried to remember. The blanket covering her mind started to fall away, and the memories started to return.

She'd been moving covertly through the Kaduna refinery.

Kosoko had caught her attention.

Abeje had been reading the people in the refinery—not too deep, just basic surface thoughts—and Kosoko's were all wrong. It wasn't just that they were bland, though they were definitely that. Still, if everyone with bland thoughts was an Oyo spy, Abeje would've had to assassinate half the population of Kaduna Township.

No, it was more than that. His thoughts were too orderly. One thing Abeje had learned early on was that the human brain didn't move in a straight line. It was more like a maze: taking multiple digressions and going into various dead-ends before getting back on track.

But Kosoko's mind didn't work like that.

That made him a person of suspicion, which meant Abeje could justify probing deeper.

When she did—she found nothing different. Kosoko's surface thoughts were all that there was.

Part of Abeje's pre-mission briefing including an intelligence report on a new psi-screen that the Oyo were developing for their covert agents, one that projected a preselected set of thoughts, so that Ori-Inu wouldn't notice them. Except, of course, the problem with preselected thoughts was that they stood out in their own way as much as totally blocking them would—to a properly trained agent, anyhow.

Amused that the Oyo had put a flawed tool into the field, Abeje followed Kosoko to the bowels of the refinery.

Processor C was one of five processors in the lower levels of the refinery. The centerpiece was a giant, forty-meter-high gray block of machinery, into which fed dozens of tubes and rolling platforms. Catwalks encircled the perimeter of all four walls at three different levels, with workstations at various points on those catwalks.

It was at one of those workstations on the third level that Abeje found Kosoko, entering data. This was a scheduled maintenance check that was on Kosoko's official itinerary for the day, according to what Abeje had downloaded from the refinery computer, but Abeje no longer needed to catch him actually committing sabotage on behalf of the Oyo rebels. His psi-screen was evidence enough for her.

Suddenly an alarm blared throughout the processor.

Kosoko yelled, *"Mogbe!"* His fingers moved more quickly across the workstation even as steam came pouring out of one of the rolling platforms.

After a moment, both the alarm and the steam stopped, though there was still a good deal of the latter hovering in the air.

"This is Kosoko," the engineer said after activating an intercom. "We've got a jam in C, but I'm clearing it now."

Someone acknowledged it on the other end.

Abeje generously waited until he was finished before she confronted him.

To her satisfaction, he jumped up about half a meter and yelped in shock when a woman in red and black body armor seemed to appear out of nowhere before him. She had used the steam to good effect, not allowing herself to be noticed until she wanted to be seen.

Her intent was to raise her Bayo and shoot the spy in the head.

But she couldn't lift her arm all of a sudden.

"Sorry to interrupt, sweets, but you and me, we got business to take care of."

Abeje whirled around, a moment's concentration being all she needed to break whatever hold was on her, and she tried to find the source of the voice that echoed off the heavy metal of the walls and the processor.

Her eyes focused on a large figure standing on the catwalk above her. The steam obscured his features, but she could make out a couple of details. One was that the weapon he carried had the exact same shape as a Cavalry-issue Ayoka rifle. The other was that, while she couldn't make out exactly what kind of clothes he was wearing, it definitely wasn't a uniform from any branch of the Cavalry.

Plus, whoever this person was, he was a telepath, if he was able to get inside her head long enough to keep her from shooting.

Now that she was aware of him, though, he wouldn't be able to pull that trick again. She fired her Bayo right at him, but by the time the round reached where he'd been standing, he was gone.

Where did he go? She reached out psionically, but she couldn't detect him.

"Look," Kosoko said, "I don't know what the hell's going on, but—"

"Shut up," Abeje said. She caught movement out of the corner of her eye and threw herself and Kosoko down to the metal surface of the catwalk just as four Ayoka rounds flew overhead.

Instinct made her protect Kosoko. Besides, he was her kill, not this other person's.

Looking up, the mystery figure was gone.

This time she closed her eyes and tried to focus, tried to find the man. She was Ori-Inu, she'd been trained how to—

"How to find another telepath, right, sweets? Yeah, I learned that, too. Not gonna work on me, though."

Abeje thought the voice was coming from below, and she shot downward with her Bayo—

—at nothing. He wasn't there.

"Who are you?"

Her question had been more or less rhetorical, but she got an answer anyhow: "I'd tell you, Abeje, but you wouldn't remember me. Once upon a time, though, we were close as can be, back when we were both training. See that trick you're trying? I learned it from the same Orisha you did."

Now Abeje thought the voice was coming from the other side of the catwalk, so she shot there, the report from the Bayo echoing off the walls even as it hit the far wall.

The steam was starting to clear, finally, but still she saw no sign of the *buruku*.

"Where are you?" she yelled. "And nice try, but you can't possibly remember whether or not we had the same Orisha. Ori-Inu are mindwiped when they finish training."

"Never said I completed the training, sweets."

This time, the voice was right behind her. Turning, Abeje saw the outline of a large figure. What frustrated her no end, though, was that she still couldn't read his mind, even though at this range she should've at least been able to get a fix on him. It wasn't that he was blocked—that was a different sensation. He wasn't wearing a screen, she just couldn't make a byte of sense out of what was in his head. It was the kind of not-quite-blank you got from an Eso—but she couldn't recall an unmodified human being like that.

"Don't call me sweets," she said through clenched teeth.

"You'll want to come with me quiet, and I won't hurt you."

"*Fimi sile!*"

"Maybe later."

Then Abeje once again found herself frozen. This was even more intense than when she couldn't kill Kosoko. No matter how hard she tried, she couldn't make herself move.

She saw the large figure looking down at the catwalk floor behind her.

From his position on the floor, Kosoko said, "Look, I don't know what's going on here, but I'm— Urk!"

In her mind, Abeje could feel that the man had done . . . *something* to Kosoko, but she had no idea what.

Then her mind went blank.

The next thing she knew, she was inside a glass tube. That same large figure was outside the tube, saying something, but she couldn't make out the words. She felt as if she couldn't breathe, even though she felt her stomach rise and fall.

Panic gripped her. She reached up and pushed against the glass that surrounded her, but to no avail. It would not budge.

The large figure moved closer, but she still couldn't make out his features. Something tickled at the back of her mind, a familiarity. She'd never seen this person before, but something . . .

Then he spoke again, but again she could not hear.

And again, her mind went blank . . .

Abeje shook her head. Being in that tube was the last thing that happened to her when she was conscious before waking up from her nightmares. Apparently, they removed the neural implant when she was in that tube.

What else did they do to me?

Blinking a few times, her night vision continued to improve.

There were bloody surgical instruments on the tables near her.

And the shapes against the wall were six tubes just like the one she briefly woke up in.

Each of them but one had a body in it.

She checked her surroundings a third time. If there were other people in here, she should damn well have sensed them.

Unless someone was using a psi-screen. But no, the only things attached to her person were the gown and the IV, and she'd ripped the latter out.

Could they have injected a psi-screen where the neural implant was?

So this time she put everything she had into psionically reading the room. With her brain less foggy, she was able to take in the entire room.

There it was. There *were* minds in this room, but they were all operating at an extremely low level. The people in those tubes were unconscious. Maybe in induced comas, or maybe just sedated so much that it reduced brain function.

Just like she had been before and after she woke up in a tube just like those others.

Are they telepaths, too? Are the Oyo taking Ori-Inu? No, that doesn't make sense, Kosoko was Oyo, and he didn't know who that person was who captured me.

Why is that buruku *so familiar?*

Swinging around, she set her feet down on the floor. The vibration of the metal beneath her bare feet confirmed that she was travelling through space. Abeje had been in enough spaceships that she could instantly tell when she was on one in transit by the vibration of the deckplates. But she had no idea how long she was out, so she didn't know how far from Oshun they were, nor where they were going.

Too many questions. Need answers.

Suddenly, a light blinded her. Holding her hand up over her face, she blinked the spots out of her eyes, trying to get her vision to clear.

Now she could clearly see the half-dozen tubes against the wall. One was empty, and she figured that was the one she'd been trapped in.

The other five, though, had people inside them, all naked.

To her shock, Abeje recognized one of them.

"Akanke?"

Abeje's stomach churned as she looked at the woman in the tube, recognizing the scar on the cheek as belonging to her fellow Ori-Inu. Akanke got the scar while fighting terrorists along with Abeje and three other Ori-Inu on Sasabonsam Station, and she'd refused to have the scar removed. "It's a good reminder of what can happen," she'd said.

A month later, she had disappeared.

Abeje had always assumed that Akanke was killed on a mission. It wasn't her place to ask for specifics.

Abeje didn't recognize the others, but she had the feeling that they were all Ori-Inu—especially since they all had the exact same scar on their right clavicles that Abeje now had, including Akanke.

"Yes," said a voice from behind her, "they all used to be Ori-Inu. But now, they're *free*."

Whirling around, Abeje saw the *buruku* who'd captured her standing in the doorway. A dark, hard face was framed by long, coarse dreadlocks tied behind his head, and he had a dark goatee. He wore a shirt, pants, and vest that all appeared to be made of leather, with bone and bead necklaces, one of which had a red pendant at the end.

How did I not sense him? Even making eye contact, she couldn't really feel his mind at all.

He was holding one of the newer Ayoka rifles, a variant on the standard-issue one. Abeje knew that variant was in development, but didn't think it was finished yet. Since Abeje was still unarmed, she didn't attack yet. She remembered her training: *The only way an unknown foe becomes a known one is by gathering information.*

"How does being operated on without your consent and then being rendered comatose in a tube make you 'free,' exactly?"

The man had a deep, throaty laugh—and, maddeningly, it just made him feel *more* familiar. "Here we go. 'The only way an unknown foe becomes a known foe is to be gatherin' intel.' You think I don't remember Hembadoon's little sayings, sweets? Don't worry, you'll know everything you need to once we reach Olokun Station."

"I told you not to call me sweets, *buruku*."

He moved briskly toward Abeje, and she immediately tensed. "I'm being rude. I keep forgetting that you don't remember me. Name's Oranmiyan." He extended his right hand, just as Abeje dove into a shoulder roll, and came up kicking at Oranmiyan's chest—

—or, rather, where Oranmiyan's chest had been when she started the roll. Oranmiyan had stepped aside and then wrapped one massive arm around Abeje's left leg, arresting her upward motion. She had intended to use the momentum from the kick to get back to her feet, but with the grab that wouldn't happen, and her head collided with the deck. The skull-jarring impact caused even more spots in her eyes than turning on the lights had.

"That was always your favorite trick during training,

sweets. Face it, you are not going to surprise me. It'll all make sense once we get to Olokun. Then you'll be free."

"You keep *saying* that!" Abeje said from the floor. Oranmiyan was still gripping her leg, and she couldn't twist out of his grip. "I'm perfectly free right now, thanks."

Oranmiyan barked a laugh. "Doing whatever Isembi tells you to do, that's your idea of free? Not hardly, sweets. You're just a program that the Hegemony's writing. But with Shango-oti, you'll be free of that."

Abeje frowned wondering what a drink of Shango—one of the old gods, and also the name of what was now the third planet, the gas giant around which Oshun and Oya orbited—would be like.

Having apparently read her thoughts, Oranmiyan grinned. "You'll see."

He let go of her leg. As soon as he did, she flipped over backwards, rolling on her right shoulder and into a ready position.

She barely saw Oranmiyan's massive fist heading for her face.

Abeje struggled to rise to her feet. So prepared had she been for another psionic attack that the sheer brutality of a punch to the face had caught her completely off guard.

Her head swam worse than it had when she woke from her nightmares and whatever drugs Oranmiyan had pumped into her fogged her.

She put one palm flat on the deck, hoping that it would gain her enough purchase to push herself to her feet.

Oranmiyan was getting closer to her. Abeje braced herself for another punch.

Instead, she felt the prick of a needle in her arm.

Oh, mogbe, *not again.*

The room started to swirl about, Oranmiyan's features growing indistinct, the tubes against the bulkhead twisting and becoming malformed, and darkness overwhelming everything . . .

. . . and she found herself walking down a corridor that was intimately familiar to her even though she'd never seen it before . . .

. . . and then she was sitting in a dining hall. Oranmiyan was there, with shorter hair and no goatee, but it was definitely him, and there was an Orisha there in his white robes and two others, a boy and a girl, and they were laughing with each other . . .

. . . and then she was back in the corridor, and a door slid open . . .

. . . and then she and the others from the dining hall were in an open field being shot at . . .

. . . and then she entered the door and there was Oranmiyan lying in a bunk and she came to him and they kissed . . .

FOUR
L'owuro

FOLAMI STARED AT THE MAN in the *L'owuro* infirmary and tried to figure out why she knew who he was.

She'd come across a few Orisha in her time. Orisha were the ones who found and trained potential Ori-Inu, but they didn't interact with them much after that training was complete, so she hadn't met all that many.

Hembadoon was not one of them.

Doctor Modupe was running a scan on him. Folami noted that Hembadoon was still wearing the white robes of his station. That surprised her at first, that Modupe had left it on, but then she recalled that Orisha robes, like Ori-Inu body armor, came with built-in first aid. Also, Orisha were high-level agents of the Hegemony. These were not people that a mere shipboard medic could disrobe with impunity.

"How is he, Doctor?"

Modupe almost leapt a meter into the air. "*Orioda*, you scared me, Folami!"

"Sorry," she lied. "I just wanted to know how he was doing."

"Physically, he should be okay. His toga, or whatever it is, kept him from dying, and I was able to stitch up the rest of it. About an hour ago, he woke up, and he's all nice and coherent, but I had to sedate him again to keep him from leaping out of bed—the man needs to *heal*, not gad about like a madman. He's going to need a week of physical therapy, but that's not the problem." Modupe shoved a reader in her face.

Folami took it, even though it was full of colored indicators that didn't actually mean anything to her.

"See that?" Modupe inexplicably expected her to recognize something in particular.

"Doctor, I—"

He snatched it back quickly. "According to every scan *L'owuro* knows how to make, Orisha Hembadoon's telepathy is at fourth level."

Folami nodded. Fifth-level was the cutoff for telepaths. Second through fourth levels often came with some kind of sensitivity to psionics, which was a handy skill for an Orisha, and indeed most were in that range. Most humans, of course, were first-level, which meant no psionic ability or sensitivity whatsoever.

Then Modupe dropped the other glove. "I checked Hembadoon's file—he's a third-level. Has been all his life."

That brought Folami up short. "Seriously?"

"Yes!" Modupe's voice cracked. "This is completely insane! Telepathy level doesn't *change!*"

"Maybe his original reading was wrong?" Even as Folami said it, she didn't sound convinced.

Modupe was quite convinced, though, as he got even shriller. "He was tested before he joined the Orisha, again after he completed his training, and again during his last physical, and *every* time, third-level!" Then he whirled on Folami. "Hold still a second, will you?" Modupe rummaged around one of the drawers set into the bulkhead of the infirmary.

As he did so, Folami looked down at Hembadoon. Modupe had gotten rid of the blood and healed the burns on the Orisha's face. She definitely knew his face quite well, even though she'd never seen him before today. She recognized his brown eyes, his rounded face, that odd shape to his nose . . .

What is going on here?

"Here."

Turning around, Folami saw Modupe holding out two small squares, which she recognized as a pair of field telepathy index readers. Even as Folami took one square from the doctor, Modupe put the other on Hembadoon's sleeping forehead. Folami did likewise with hers; it adhered to her flesh instantly.

Modupe then entered a command into his handheld unit, and Folami felt a dozen or so tiny needles prick through her skin and hit the bone of her skull. His brow furrowed, the doctor scratched the thatch of hair on his left cheek while he waited.

After a second, the needles retracted. Even though Folami didn't reach for it, Modupe yelled, "*Don't* take it off, yet! It needs to stop the bleedi—"

"This isn't my first time using one of these," Folami said testily. "Well?"

"See for yourself." Modupe held up the unit display-out. Dark blue on a pale blue background provided the following: **subject 1: 4. subject 2: 10.**

"Assuming I was subject two," Folami said dryly, "it's accurate."

"Of course you were! I just don't understand it!"

Folami, however, was having thoughts in that direction.

Before she could articulate them, the intercom sounded. "Ori-Inu, report to War Chief Tobi's cabin immediately."

Now she took the square off her forehead. The pinprick

wounds in her head had healed over, and the blood wiped away (even minor head wounds bled profusely). Dropping it on the nearest table, she headed for the exit, ignoring Modupe's complaining about how she could have just handed it to him.

I'm starting to understand why nobody likes him.

She sauntered through the corridors of *L'owuro.* Everyone avoided getting too close to her, some going so far as to push themselves against the bulkheads.

Filthy buruku, *(I bet it'd) I can't believe they let (be great with her.) her just walk (She's probably) the corridors (reading my mind) like that. I'm glad she's here, (right now!!!!) but does she (I hope) have to be (they have the) such a beautiful (meat loaf tonight.) girl? I (I love) don't want (the meat) a protector (loaf) I want (with bacon) to fuck.*

It was the curse of being tenth-level. She didn't pry—even if it was legal, just the thought of it made her almost break out in hives—but she couldn't keep out the obvious strong emotional thoughts. The cavalry and support staff who walked the corridors of *L'owuro* right now had *very* emotional thoughts, and the only ones that weren't negative thoughts directed at her came from the one—one of the cavalry chiefs—with the meat-loaf-and-bacon fetish.

Turning a corridor led her to the cul-de-sac which ended with the war chief's cabin. Before even approaching the door, she sensed two minds inside, one of which was scared witless.

Definitely not Tobi, Folami thought with a smile. The war chief didn't do fear. Folami figured that would lead him to do something spectacularly stupid in the field one day. Tobi was generally good enough that his inability to let fear temper his reactions didn't matter all that much. But Folami figured it was only a matter of time.

I just have to hope he's got a different Ori-Inu assigned to him when it does happen.

The steel door to the cabin slid aside at her approach, which meant that the war chief had programmed the door to recognize her and let her in, something he'd never done before.

Tobi kept his desk facing the front door from a distance of only a couple of meters, so his face was the first thing you saw when you came into his cabin. Right now that face was scowling. He was in his dress uniform, which was also unusual, and might have been the reason for the scowl, since Tobi probably would have chosen to again go out in a dashiki with nothing under it than his dress reds.

The war chief sat behind his desk, his massive form framed by the dozens of weapons that hung on the wall behind him. Folami recognized all of them, various models by Ayoka and Bayo, as well as a few by Oledele, even though his designs weren't favored much these days.

Very little was on the desk itself: a standard terminal, two data readers, and nothing else.

The source of the fear she had felt outside was the young cavalryman standing next to Tobi. Based on Folami's surface read, the young man had never been summoned to Tobi's presence before, and he probably would have lived a much happier life if he'd gone through it without that particular experience. The cavalryman's hairline was receding, and his high forehead was glistening with sweat. His hands were clasped tensely behind his back in a largely futile attempt to hide his nervousness.

"Reporting as ordered," Folami said with a salute. Since they were outside the military rank structure—or above it, depending on who one asked—Ori-Inu weren't required to salute anyone, but Folami always did so anyhow.

If Tobi appreciated it, he had yet to show it. He simply returned the salute and said, "Cavalryman, report to the Ori-Inu."

The junior officer swallowed audibly. "Uhm, well, we completed the atmospheric analysis on the battle site. There was, ah, some kind of—of, well, gas that was released in the initial explosion that—that the computer didn't, uh, didn't recognize. Entirely."

Folami frowned. "That was a Kaduna refinery, wasn't it?"

"Yes, ma'am. And I, ah, I checked the scans against everything Kaduna has on—on record. Unfortunately, whatever this stuff is, it disperses pretty, uh—well, pretty quickly. From the time you and Rufiji hit dirt to when you did that thing with the Eso, the concentration went down from—from eighty parts per million to two parts per *trillion*. We don't even have a proper—proper sample. We re-ran the scans four times to be—to be sure, but the results were the same every time."

Tobi stared at Folami the entire time that the cavalryman spoke with what the war chief had probably hoped was a penetrating stare. It had yet to faze Folami.

"Thank you, Cavalryman, that'll be all."

"Thank you, sir." He practically ran past Folami to the door. A first-level could have detected his relief at being excused.

As soon as the door slid shut, Tobi activated the holoviewer on his desk, which then provided an image of Orisha Hembadoon, along with the abstract from a classified file. "This," the war chief said, "is your Orisha buddy's mission. He was investigating Ori-Inu who've been disappearing."

Folami's eyes widened. "I'm sorry?"

"Not only that, but it's a level-seven mission straight from the Oba."

Smiling, Folami said, "I was wondering why you were wearing the first-class uni."

"Yeah." In one drawn-out syllable, Tobi managed to pack a great deal of disdain for Oba Isembi's protocol that all line officers report to him in dress uniforms when practical. "That's why you're here. We need to report to Oba Isembi. As soon as the flight deck has the signal, they'll let us know."

Tobi rose to his feet, then, and moved toward the sideboard that was under the collection of weapons. He snatched a thick-bottomed glass from the lower shelf and poured an amber liquid from an etched glass carafe. Then the war chief turned to scowl at Folami, and she could read that thought loud and clear: *Go ahead,* buruku, *wait for me to offer you a drink.*

"War Chief," Folami said with a sigh, "if you want to intimidate me, I have a suggestion: make your skin chitinous, replace your hands and feet with claws, and take your orders from Oyo rebels. Otherwise, you're just wasting your energy."

Tobi had poured himself a sour mash from back home on Ife, and he slugged it down before responding. "Why would I try to intimidate *you*? That would be like trying to intimidate this glass of booze—or my pistol. You're just another tool, Ori-Inu. I'm thinking you need some help reading people. You're getting intimidation mixed up with contempt."

Folami's retort was interrupted by the voice of the Eji-shift communications officer. "Flight deck to War Chief Tobi."

Sitting back down at his desk, Tobi touched a control on his terminal. "Tobi."

"Oba Isembi is ready for his audience with you, War Chief."

Tobi, based on both his expression and surface thoughts, didn't think much of the protocol that forced the officer to refer to a communication from Ife in such a manner, either.

"Put him through, Cavalryman."

"Yes, sir."

The image projected by the holoviewer on the desk changed from that of Hembadoon to that of the Hegemony's monarch. Folami had long admired the man, and even met him a few times, and she never failed to be impressed by his presence. She often wondered how it was that Tobi managed to convince people to follow him into battle, but such questions had never occurred to her regarding the Oba.

Without preamble, Isembi asked, "Where's Orisha Hembadoon?"

"Still unconscious, my Oba," Folami said, her head inclined slightly out of respect.

"However," Tobi said, "the last report he filed on his ship indicated he was going to talk to someone named Kosoko, who was the last person the Ori-Inu he was looking for was seen talking to. The dead body we found nearest to the Orisha was identified as having that same name."

Isembi gritted his teeth. "I assume, War Chief, that you've read the Orisha's mission profile?"

"Just now, my Oba."

"Good, because as of now, you're attached to it. Folami, so are you. Until the Orisha regains consciousness, you are to take over his investigation. I want to find out where my Ori-Inu have gone."

"Sir, there's more," Folami said before Tobi could speak. She hadn't intended to overwrite him like that, but it was done. "The explosion that injured Orisha Hembadoon—and killed Kosoko, for that matter—released a gas into the atmosphere. The *L'owuro* lab couldn't identify it."

"What kind of— No, you said that your lab couldn't identify it."

"We do know that the gas has some kind of effect on telepathic ability, my Oba. According to the ship's doctor, Orisha Hembadoon's psionic level has gone up a full level."

Isembi's thick eyebrows raised at that. "Really?"

Folami nodded. "It also—I think it might have affected me as well."

"In what way?"

"Weird flashes of—of things I don't remember." The next sentence came out of Folami's mouth practically unbidden. "Probably hallucinations of some kind."

She managed to control her reaction to her own words. But she also lied to the Oba. For some reason, she thought it was *critically* important that Oba Isembi not know that she was regaining old memories. She knew that she'd been mindwiped upon completion of her training. She was permitted to remember that training, but not anything else that came before. Ori-Inu did the job better if they were unencumbered by their previous lives.

Folami was morally certain that the flashes she'd gotten in the field were from that erased past. If it came to that, that was probably how she knew Orisha Hembadoon—as like as not, he was the one who recruited and trained her.

So why don't I want Oba Isembi to know about it?

She shoved the question into the back of her mind, and finished her report. "The gas doesn't match anything currently being produced by the Kaduna facilities, nor is it a naturally occurring gas."

"I want to know what this gas is. I've already diverted all the Ori-Inu within a day's travel of Oshun to you—Folami, I hereby appoint you to be the senior in the field. Full interrogation methods are authorized."

Being senior in the field meant that, for this mission, all the Ori-Inu reported to her. The authorization meant she and the other Ori-Inu could scan all they wanted to anyone considered a significant person in the investigation, as long as they could justify it after the fact.

"War Chief, I want daily progress reports from you. *L'owuro* is to be the center point for the investigation. When the Ori-Inu arrive, find accommodations for them—either on your ship or commandeered space on the surface. The Ori-Inu are authorized to use Orisha priority."

"Understood."

"Yes, sir."

"War Chief Tobi, I want my Ori-Inu back. And I want to know why a gas that alters telepathy levels is being manufactured without my knowledge. If these wants are not satisfied, I will hold you personally responsible. You do not wish to disappoint me."

Once Isembi's visage faded from the holoviewer, Tobi glared at Folami. "Mind telling me when you were planning on sharing the information about the gas with me?"

"I only just found out before you summoned me here."

"I don't appreciate being sideswiped like that, Ori-Inu."

Feigning confusion, Folami asked, "What difference does it make? You were going to find out anyhow—this way I only had to explain it once."

Tobi started to speak, but Folami really didn't feel like being on the receiving end of his abuse any longer.

"It's going to take them some time to get themselves together on the surface, and I'd rather not interrupt the cleanup efforts after the mess we made. Besides, I want to give Orisha Hembadoon a chance to wake up so we don't repeat any of his work—and the other Ori-Inu won't be here until tomorrow. So I won't need any of your people until tomorrow at the earliest."

With that, Folami turned and left Tobi's presence.

Even as she departed, she was surprised at her own haughtiness. She was acting perfectly within her rights as an Ori-Inu. Not only didn't she report to Tobi, but he was pretty much her chauffeur when he wasn't being combat support. Still, she'd never been so dismissive of a cavalry commander before.

I have got to find out what that gas was.

Folami was still exhausted from the fight against the Eso, so she headed straight to her own cabin.

Turning the corner, she felt a familiar set of thoughts, and then saw the face that went with them. Unlike the other personnel on board, this one didn't go out of his way to avoid her. Instead, the smiling face and near-bald head of Adejola met her head-on.

"Folami! How are you? Feeling better after your workout with the Eso?"

Chuckling, Folami said, "More than a workout, but yeah, I'm fine. I was just going to study my eyelids for a while."

She could feel his disappointment in that, which confused her. "That's too bad," he said, words mirroring thoughts.

"Why?"

"Well, I was all set to invite you to join me for dinner."

Folami's confusion only deepened. "Why would you want to do that?"

Adejola laughed. "Why wouldn't I? You're a beautiful woman, an interesting conversationalist, and I want to get to know you better. Inviting you to dinner seems to me like the obvious next step."

"I'm Ori-Inu," she said slowly.

"Yeah, so?"

Folami blinked. Intellectually, she knew that people who were interested in each other dined together. But nobody had ever been interested in her enough to ask—or if they were, they were too intimidated to ask. Generally, when she shared her meals with anyone, it was either other Ori-Inu or a cavalry company she was attached to that had limited mess facilities. A one-on-one dinner was simply out of her range of experiences.

That she remembered, anyhow. Though whatever new memories that gas on Oshun had squeezed forward didn't seem to include anything like this.

A term did suddenly leap into her brain: date. Adejola was asking her out on a date.

"Look," Adejola said, "every time I go out with a woman, there's always a certain—well, frustration with her inability to get what I'm thinking. I figure with you, that won't be an issue."

At that, Folami barked out a laugh. "I don't know if I should mix business with pleasure."

That got Adejola to laugh, and she realized that he had done so in her presence twice. It was exceedingly rare to find a flatbrain who laughed with her.

Another thought came to her, and that was the one that convinced her to say yes: If Tobi found out, he'd be furious.

"All right," Folami said. "Shall we proceed to the mess hall, Cavalry Chief?"

"I was hoping for something more private. Maybe your quarters—this way you're on safe ground."

That brought Folami up short. There was no shortage of cavalry on this vessel of both sexes whose dream was to be inside Folami's quarters, and not to share a meal. But if Adejola had such a desire, he kept it tamped down fairly well.

And he was right, it was her own territory, so she could set the rules.

Plus, she was an Ori-Inu, and he was just a pilot. If he tried anything untoward, she'd be able to kill him without even trying very hard.

The dinner that Folami and Adejola shared was not the best—it was still prepared by the same chef who made all the mediocre meals on *L'owuro*—but it was still the finest Folami had had in a long time.

Adejola spent a lot of time talking about himself. "Believe it or not, I never wanted to be a pilot. Every other spacehopper I've ever met has been completely locked into that, that they just *had* to be a pilot, like it's a drug."

"But not you?" Folami asked.

Shaking his head, Adejola said, "Nope. I mean, I was always good at it. Me and some friends back home on Ife, we took flying lessons one year for fun. See, I grew up with four other friends, and one of them, Egba, was kind of the pack leader, y'know? *She* was one of the types who always wanted to fly. The other four of us kinda got sucked up into it with her."

"So you all took lessons?" Folami asked after sipping the awful wine that was all Tobi had allowed in the cargo hold. The war chief said that decision was based on the notion that the cavalry were less likely to show up on duty drunk if the only option was bad wine. In practice, the notion hadn't worked out so well. A cavalry who was determined to drink would take whatever was available. Knowing Tobi, Folami assumed that he figured if cavalry *were* going to get drunk, they were going to suffer for it by drinking vinegar.

"Yeah, and I was the only one who took to it. Poor Egba was

a *terrible* pilot. No aptitude for it, and she had depth-perception issues."

Folami frowned. "She had a depth-perception problem and she wanted to *fly*?"

"We didn't know she had it, or we would've stopped her."

"How could she not know she had it?" Folami knew that there were those on the colony worlds who did not have access to even the most basic medical care, but that was rare on Ife itself, particularly with someone who could afford piloting lessons.

Adejola chuckled. "I said *we* didn't know, not that *she* didn't know."

Folami shook her head. "I will never understand that."

"Understand what?"

After sipping her wine, and almost choking it down, she replied. "Dangerous self-delusion. It's one thing to strive for something that's difficult, but to ignore something your body's incapable of . . . I just don't understand it."

"Well, as a telepath, you're a lot more aware of what your body can and can't do. Egba, she'd never *needed* depth-perception before. Not really."

"So she failed?"

"Never even made it that far—they wouldn't let her into the simulator once they scanned her. She got completely crazy over it and wanted to just turn around and leave. But the rest of us had already paid our fee, so we went on with the lessons." He sipped some wine also, then winced before continuing. "At the end of it all, she wasn't speaking to any of us because we 'betrayed' her, and I got a rating of fifteen."

While Folami had no idea what that rating meant, she could tell from the manner in which Adejola said it and from the pride in his thoughts that his fifteen rating was akin to her being a tenth-level telepath. "So you pursued it?"

"Honestly, I was seventeen, I had no idea what I wanted to do with my life, and suddenly I found something I was good at. Plus, my other friends, even though they went through with what they paid for, eventually took Egba's side. They all thought I betrayed their trust by signing up for a formal piloting school."

"That's madness!"

Adejola shrugged. "Way I see it, if they were willing to end the friendship over that—if Egba's being happy was more important than my being happy—then it wasn't a friendship worth salvaging."

"So you joined the cavalry?"

"Not exactly—I did private jobs, at first. But this was back before the war, and a lot of my clients were Oyo. Once Yemoja blew up, work was harder to come by, so I let myself be recruited by the Cavalry."

Folami smiled. "I can imagine." But something nagged at the back of her mind. When he'd referred to Yemoja blowing up, Folami had felt her heart skip a beat. It made no sense— unless, perhaps, she'd been to Yemoja before its destruction?

The conversation went on from there, and by the time they got to dessert—a near-tasteless cocoa cake—Folami asked the question that had been on her mind since Adejola had first talked to her on the flight deck.

"Cavalry Chief, why did you ask me on this date?"

Another laugh. Folami decided she liked his laugh. "I'll tell you, but you have to agree to call me Adejola."

She smiled. "Okay, Adejola, why did you ask me—"

"Because I wanted to get to know *you*. Everyone treats you like a weapon or an object, and I don't think that's fair. I guess I got used to that from when I was working commissions. Nobody paid any attention to me, I was just a part of the machinery."

"And you didn't like that feeling, I take it?"

"No." Adejola leaned forward. "I see you being treated the same way, and I don't like it. You're a *person*, no more a part of the machinery than I was. I figured you should be treated like one."

Folami popped the last of the awful cake into her mouth, looked at Adejola, and smiled, saying, "Thank you for that, Adejola."

And she meant it. The notion of being treated like other people was as completely outside her range of previous experience as a date was, and she found that she liked both a great deal.

FIVE
Oshun

ABAMETA WAS THE OLDEST ACTIVE Ori-Inu. He took considerable pride in this accomplishment, as being an Ori-Inu wasn't a profession that lent itself to longevity.

But no matter how many missions he went on—and he'd been on so many he'd long since lost count—he always managed to survive.

Now he was pushing forty. While most humans would consider this only a third of the way through their lives, most Ori-Inu didn't even see their thirtieth birthdays.

He wasn't sure what it was he had that the other Ori-Inu didn't. He was a sixth-level—not the most powerful, nor the weakest telepath in the bunch—he was a perfectly good fighter, and had decent aim with his rifle. Other Ori-Inu, with far more skill or higher ratings had died around him.

The call to divert to Oshun had come while he was on his way back to Ife for a new assignment. He'd hired a civilian transport to take him home, so he simply instructed the shipmaster to change course.

Abameta had heard about the infamous Folami, but had assumed it all to be hyperbole and rumor. Certainly, she couldn't have been as beautiful as everyone said she was. In Abameta's experience, most Ori-Inu were like him: craggy, weathered, scarred, and cynical.

As ordered, he reported to *L'owuro*, heading straight for the vessel's wardroom once the civilian transport dropped him off. The other eleven Ori-Inu were already present, and they were simply awaiting the mission's leader.

After Abameta had been sitting for ten minutes, the doors to the wardroom parted, and a strikingly tall woman entered.

To his shock, Abameta discovered that Folami was just what everyone said she was. Beyond her impressive height, she had a toned, hourglass figure, which was complimented by her standard-issue red-and-black body armor. That, at least, was to be expected, as one didn't last long as an Ori-Inu without being in near-perfect shape. Her hair was cut short, but not all the way to the scalp. Amazingly, despite the fact that she'd been on dozens of missions, several of which she'd been the only survivor of, her face was unblemished.

Something else the rumor mill missed was her intelligent obsidian eyes.

Folami took her seat at the head of the wardroom table and activated a holograph in the table's center. It showed an image of a fiery wreckage of what had once been an industrial complex of some sort.

"This is the mission," Folami said. "A half-dozen of our fellow Ori-Inu have gone missing over the past few months. The latest was Abeje. When Orisha Hembadoon was sent to investigate, this Kaduna Mining Corporate refinery that you see here was destroyed. The Orisha is still unconscious in the *L'owuro* infirmary. The refinery explosion released an as-yet-unidentified gas into the atmosphere. Oyo rebels have claimed responsibility, and did attack Kaduna Township upon our arrival, which tracks with what we downloaded from the Orisha's robe computer. The Oyo spy that Abeje was tracking was the one who blew the place up.

"Your missions are to patrol the hospitals, the area around the refinery, and Kaduna Station. We have authority to fully scan *anyone* we consider a significant person in this investigation. Be careful—" Those intense black eyes suddenly felt as if they were boring right into Abameta's head. "—because you will be asked to justify any scans in your after-action reports."

Abameta noted several of the other Ori-Inu squirming in their seats. He just smiled. Such authorizations used to be more common, but Isembi had decided recently to at least create the illusion of benevolence by tightening the restrictions on deep scans. Abameta had been on one mission a year ago where a fellow Ori-Inu had scanned a civilian bystander in order to find a particular location. Said bystander found out about it and reported the Ori-Inu in question. That Ori-Inu's name had been absent from the active roster ever since.

Folami finished: "Your specific areas of investigation have been uploaded to your armor computers. Send me daily reports, please, as I'm reporting straight to the Oba on this one."

More murmurs around the table, but Abameta's voice wasn't among them. If it was worth dragging a dozen Ori-Inu to a single planet and if it involved an unknown gas produced by a refinery, it had to be big.

In fact, Abameta was pretty sure that the gas was of far greater import than the missing Ori-Inu. While Oba Isembi made a public fuss about how important each of his special agents was, Abameta had been at this far too long to believe that. They were all interchangeable parts, all lines in the program code of Isembi's master plan.

A dropship took ten of the Ori-Inu to Oshun's surface. Folami remained on board *L'owuro* to coordinate, while the remaining two went to Kaduna Station to see if anyone knew anything about a ship that had taken the missing Ori-Inu.

The Ori-Inu seated next to Abameta on the dropship was a tall, gangly boy who wouldn't stop talking.

"This is *so* hyped! *This* is what it's all about, am I right, huh, am I?"

Abameta scowled at the child. "Being an Ori-Inu is all about doing what you're told."

"Well, *yeah*, sure it is, but I mean, come *on*, this—finding a lost Ori-Inu, solving a mystery, scanning folks . . ."

"You ever scanned anyone, child?" Abameta asked. He tried to keep the pity out of his voice, but didn't succeed very well to his own ears.

"Well, I mean, in training, but . . . Well, what's the hype, anyhow? I mean, so we read a couple folks more than normal, right?"

Abameta shook his head. "The human mind is a swamp, child. It's dirty and muck-encrusted, filled with all kinds of garbage that you do not see coming, and when you're done, it's damn near impossible to get it off you. And this mission? We have to do it *over and over* again. Think about everything that a person has seen, heard, *experienced*. Then you have to sift through *all* of that to see if there's anything that's actually germane to the mission. And *then* you have to put it out of your mind—which you cannot do completely—and move on to the next person."

The boy just stared at Abameta for a few seconds.

Then he shook his head. "Maybe for an old man like you, but me? I can handle that with *no* flaws."

To Abameta's relief, the boy ignored him the rest of the trip down.

Abameta's assignment was one of the hospitals that had taken in those injured by the refinery explosion.

He started with the ones in the burn unit. Most of them were sedated, which meant that there wouldn't be much there to read. Of course, the downside of that was that there was probably a lot that Abameta wouldn't be able to read at all, but it was worth the risk.

He moved silently through the Dada Memorial Hospital. According to the text that accompanied a holograph on display in the hospital lobby, the facility had been named after the doctor who founded it back when Oshun was first colonized.

Out of curiosity, Abameta looked up Doctor Dada on his computer, only to discover that the doctor had died in disgrace, bankrupt and miserable, thanks to a botched operation that left both a woman and her unborn child dead following what should have been a routine repair of a damaged bone.

As he approached the burn unit, Abameta had to chuckle to himself. The real story was always more interesting to him than the legend, which made him wonder where the legends came from, since they were *supposed* to be the better stories . . .

The first person he came upon was a maintenance worker.

Ow (What was that?) this (Need more overtime.) hurts. (I hate her.) Ow (Never should've) this (married her.) hurts. (What was that?) Ow (Hope our team wins this week.) this (Stupid woman, annoying me.) hurts. (Never should've) Ow (What was that?) this (married her.) hurts. (Leave me alone, woman!) Ow (Gotta get that money he owes me.) this (Never should've married her.) hurts. (What was that?)

Abameta shuddered. *There but for the grace of telepathy, go I,* he thought. If he hadn't been a telepath, he probably would've spent his life as a nobody like this sad specimen.

He moved onto the next one—another maintenance worker, this one a supervisor.

What's (I have to) going (Where'd he go?) on? (make that payment.) Where (If he doesn't) am (come back,) I? (I need the overtime.) Why (I'll kill him.) is this (Have to get that present) happening? (for the boys.) Help me!

Next was one of another drudge.

Hope the (I love you.) company covers (I love you.) this. Hope she (I love you.) doesn't use this (I can sell this.) as an excuse (I love you.) to sleep (I bet the information net will pay a ton.) around. Hope (I love you.) I can get a (This'll be my pass off this rock.) good deal (I love you.) for this.

By the time he reached the final person, Abameta was ready to throw himself out a high-story window. *These people's lives are so dull*, he thought with disgust. All they cared about was money and their own little, pointless lives.

The last one, though, was a technician, the first non-menial staff member Abameta had come across.

Must protect (Help me!) the experiments. (They're all dying!) Must protect (It hurts!) the (The fire's everywhere!) scientists. Must (Someone please, help me!) protect the (I can't feel my legs!) computers. (The Shango-oti!) Must protect (It hurts so much!) the project. Ojiji (No! No! No!) must go (My body's on fire!) on, or they'll (Help me!) kill me. (I'm dying!)

That got Abameta's attention instantly. There was an intensity here that was missing from the others, especially given that—unlike the others—the anxiety this one felt was unrelated to his own injuries. Plus the terms *Shango-oti* and *Ojiji* jumped out at him.

Closing his eyes, he probed deeper.

Ojiji must go on.

Fabayo's gonna kill me!

Oh, mogbe, *does this hurt!*

Why won't they make the pain go away?

The Shango-oti is getting loose!

Someone call Fabayo, he'll need to tell his bosses about this!

Abameta smiled.

Oranmiyan sighed as he looked down at Abeje's supine form on the deck. He had been hoping that she would go down without a fight.

He should have known better. However, the sedative he gave her did its job.

For a minute, Oranmiyan just stared at her. *It's been so long . . .*

Abeje had perfect cheekbones and lips that were both full and pouty. Oranmiyan clearly remembered the taste of those lips. Right now, her straight brown hair was tied back in a ponytail, but Oranmiyan would always remember it splayed sloppily across the pillow after they made love.

The hospital gown she wore did nothing to compliment her lean figure, but it had shifted enough that Oranmiyan could see her toned arms. She was in even better shape than when last he saw her.

Oranmiyan knew Abeje a lot better than she knew herself. He was the one who taught her the forward and backward rolls during their training. Oranmiyan had quit the training before the end, once he realized what the Hegemony really was. In fact, leaving Abeje behind was his only real regret.

When Hembadoon first recruited him, he wouldn't have even *needed* mindwiping. He had been as patriotic a citizen of the Olodumare Hegemony as one could imagine, ready, willing, and eager to do whatever was necessary to protect the Hegemony from its enemies.

He was younger, then, and more foolish. That fateful day when he'd encountered that Eso super-soldier changed everything. For the first time, his mind was opened.

And for the first time, his mind was closed. After mindlinking with that experimental super-soldier—the only one of its kind, and one it took three trainees, Hembadoon, and two full-fledged Ori-Inu to bring down—other telepaths couldn't read Oranmiyan, and mindwiping stopped working. Oranmiyan had no love for the Oyo rebels, and had happily killed dozens of them both before and after his fateful mindlink, but he was grateful for whatever it was that that one experiment had done to him.

But what he learned from that mindlink destroyed the entire world that Oranmiyan had spent his life believing was the real one. He quit training, letting them think he was dead, and then moved on.

Since the discovery of Shango-oti, he knew that all Ori-Inu could enjoy the freedom that he had gained. Freedom to think. Freedom to fulfill their potential, not be stifled by Isembi's rules and regulations.

Freedom to *act*.

Bending to his knees, Oranmiyan gently picked up Abeje's sleeping form and brought her out of the room.

Soon she would be introduced to the wonders of Shango-oti.

And then she would be free, and they'd be together again.

It was in the middle of Eji-shift when Folami had compiled her report for the Oba.

Arriving on the flight deck, she saw that the command chair was empty, which meant the war chief wasn't on deck.

She called up the crew roster on her suit's computer, and found that Cavalry Master Ama was second-in-command of Eji-shift. She was currently staffing the tactical station.

"I need to speak to War Chief Tobi," Folami said without preamble.

Ama's contempt for Ori-Inu seeped through her every thought—not to mention the look of disgust she gave Folami. "He's not here."

With that, she turned back to her station.

Folami sighed. "Look, Cavalry Master, I don't care about your brother being recruited as an Ori-Inu or the fact that he got killed during a training exercise. Lots of people get killed in training exercises. It has nothing to do with me, or this mission, so kindly stop being a fool."

Now Ama grinned. "Oh, I was hoping you'd throw my brother in my face. See, he isn't in my service record, which means you got that by scanning me—and you can't do that. Wanna just report to the brig now?"

The cavalry master's glee at being able to punish someone for what happened to her brother hit Folami like a slap.

So she slapped back. "Sorry, Cavalry Master, but right now I'm on a priority mission from the Oba. I need to talk to the war chief so we can report our progress to Ife, and for the duration of this mission, I've been given extreme latitude on who I can scan. So unless you want me to start telling the rest of the shift what your taste in music is, which actor you hoard images of, and what you did at that pond when you were six, I suggest you tell me where the war chief is."

Ama's face fell, and Folami could feel the nervousness

cascade across Eji-shift like a wave, because as soon as Folami left the flight deck, the cavalry master was going to take out her frustrations on her underlings.

Well, too bad. She should've just told me where the war chief is. Normally, Folami would never have been so cavalier with other people's thoughts, particularly those of her support. But she'd had enough of Ama's wholly unjustified superior attitude. Also, the report she had to give the Oba was urgent.

Through clenched teeth, Ama said, "The war chief is in his cabin."

"Thank you," Folami said with an exaggerated bow.

Then she thought about it, and decided to put her tenth-level to good use.

Closing her eyes, she concentrated, and temporarily shut down the minds of everyone on the flight deck, except for Cavalry Master Ama. Then she focused on each person's memory center.

After about half a minute, she opened her eyes. Ama was staring at her with fury.

"Calm down, Cavalry Master, I just did you a favor. All eight people on this flight deck no longer remember me coming in here and dressing you down, and no longer remember my bringing up potentially embarrassing facts from your past. Your authority is untarnished."

Ama simply glared at her, speechless.

Folami stepped close enough to Ama to smell the reconstituted eggs she'd had for breakfast. "Remember this favor the next time you decide to play games with an Ori-Inu. I could've done a lot more harm to you—instead I helped you. Because that's what I'm *supposed* to do, and what you're supposed to do for me."

Turning her back on the cavalry master, she said, "I assume I won't be seeing any reports on my scan from you."

Not waiting for an answer, she concentrated and released her hold on the flight deck crew.

Leaving it to Ama to explain the subjective jump in time they'd all experienced, Folami took her second trip to Tobi's cabin. She had had to go to the flight deck in the first place because he'd gone quiet on communications. In all likelihood he was engaged in some manner of classified communiqué—but Folami's business superseded any other business he had right now.

This time, when she approached the door, it didn't slide open, and the screen to the door's right indicated that the privacy seal was on. The screen also indicated that Tobi had been made aware of her presence.

So she waited.

She sensed nothing but Tobi's normal thoughts on the other side. He didn't seem overly concerned—in fact, he was rather relaxed, and thinking about what he was going to have to drink.

Obviously, he wasn't involved in any kind of classified business, so Folami instructed the computer to override the seal, using the Orisha priority she'd been granted by the Oba.

The door slid aside to reveal Tobi sitting at his desk, his head framed by his weapons collection, a drink in his hand. He was in his regular uniform. Protocol meant that he would have to change into his dress uniform to speak with Isembi, but Folami suspected that the Oba wouldn't want to wait for this report.

"Let me guess," Tobi said, "you have a report for the Oba?"

"Good guess," Folami said with a wry smile as she entered

the cabin, the door sliding shut behind her.

"You wouldn't have broken my seal for any other reason. That's one of the few things I like about you, Ori-Inu, you don't abuse your privileges."

Folami considered and rejected the notion of thanking him for the uncharacteristic compliment, instead getting right down to business. "We need to contact Ife immediately. And we shouldn't wait until you change—I've gotten the reports from the Ori-Inu on the ground, and it's not good."

"It wasn't especially likely to be." Tobi stabbed at a control on his desk. "Flight deck, this is Tobi."

"Flight deck."

"Cavalrywoman, set up the link to the Oba."

"Yes, sir."

Folami read what Tobi was thinking. Once this mission got underway, Tobi knew that instant communication with Oba Isembi might be vital, so he had the communications department and the Oba's technicians on Ife coordinate their efforts to provide a near-instant link between *L'owuro* and the Oba for the duration of the mission.

"Nice work," Folami said aloud.

Tobi snorted. "It's called being good at my job." He pointed at his rank insignia. "They don't just give these out for hanging around for a long time."

The flight deck came back. "Oba Isembi is ready for his audience with you, War Chief."

Tobi activated his holoviewer, which once again displayed the visage of the Oba.

"Shall I take it from the looks on your faces that you do not have good news?" Isembi asked sourly.

"I'm afraid not, my Oba," Folami said with a sigh. She had

been hoping her face wouldn't be so easily read. However, the Oba had always preferred respectful honesty to falsehood, especially in matters in which he had taken a personal interest. "Report."

"There are several people at the Kaduna Mining Corporate who are working on a secret operation called Ojiji. We've scanned half a dozen people, ranging from technicians and scientists to support staff, who work for this project. There is no mention of Ojiji in any official records either for Kaduna or anywhere else in the Hegemony."

That last sentence was said with a particular emphasis. She was hoping that this would turn out to be some kind of covert program the Oba had set up.

However, Isembi's next words, spoke with considerable venom, dashed that hope. "I've never heard of this—this 'Ojiji'."

Tobi then asked, "What's this project doing, exactly?"

Folami shot the war chief a look. He seemed genuinely curious about it, which surprised her. In Folami's experience, Tobi had never seemed the inquisitive type.

She said, "They're refining a gas called Shango-oti. Unsurprisingly, given the effects on Orisha Hembadoon, we've determined that it's a vapor designed to increase someone's telepathic abilities."

"And who exactly is running this project?"

With another sigh, Folami said, "We don't know. The local supervisor was a geologist named Fabayo, but he was just the point person at this refinery. He wasn't running the project, and he never told anyone who it was he reported to—said it was classified." Folami didn't bother to add that many of those scanned on the subject were somewhat bitter that they were kept unaware of the final authority over Ojiji.

She went on: "Unfortunately, Fabayo himself died in the explosion. His personnel record doesn't mention Ojiji, but it does mention that he was single, no living relatives, no friends. He was born on Ife, but he's lived all over the system since he got his doctorate—he went where the work was, and his work was focused entirely on geology."

"Ori-Inu," Tobi said impatiently, "the Oba doesn't need to know all that."

"On the contrary, War Chief," Isembi said with a small smile, "Folami is making it clear that Fabayo is a dead end, investigatively speaking. She is demonstrating her thoroughness in attempting to determine what, exactly, this rogue project is. I appreciate that."

After making a sidelong glance at Tobi, who was scowling, Folami continued. "My Oba, as far as we can tell, everyone who worked on Ojiji except for Fabayo assumed it to be legitimate. With your permission, I'd like to wait until Orisha Hembadoon regains consciousness before proceeding. We don't know how far he got in interrogating Kosoko."

"What does that have to do with anything?" Tobi snapped.

"According to the autopsy done on Kosoko, he had a transmitter implanted in his heart—a dead man's switch, which was linked to the explosive that destroyed the refinery."

"Abeje's mission was to track down an Oyo spy," Isembi said. "Obviously this Kosoko person was her target."

"Yeah," Tobi said, "but Hembadoon's report had him in prison—and gone completely insane. Anyhow, he's not likely to be part of this Ojiji."

Folami frowned, less at Tobi's tone, which she was used to, but his apparent surety that Kosoko wasn't connected to Ojiji. "Even so," she said, "his attack on the refinery may have been related to Ojiji."

"Don't be ridiculous. He was Oyo, like the Oba just said."

"If you two would like to continue this argument in private . . ." Isembi said still wearing the small smile, but now with a deadly undertone.

Folami straightened. Arguing in front of the Oba wasn't the wisest move for either of them—though, typically, Tobi didn't seem all that concerned. "Apologies, my Oba."

Isembi waved a hand as if he were swatting an insect. "No matter. The important thing now is to find out what happened to Abeje and who runs this Ojiji."

"Yes, sir," Folami said. "We—"

A double-toned klaxon blared through Tobi's cabin, the first tone long, the second short. That indicated an Orisha priority signal, which was just about the only circumstance under which the flight deck would interrupt this conversation.

"Sir, apologies for the interruption, but we're receiving an emergency call from the Ori-Inu on the surface."

"Which one?" Folami asked.

"All of them."

Tobi glanced at Isembi's image, and the Oba quickly said, "By all means, War Chief."

"Put it through, Cavalrywoman."

"Yes, War Chief. The signal's weak, though."

The cavalrywoman's words were proven correct a second later, as static blared through the speakers in Tobi's cabin. ". . . emergen . . . need backup immed . . . to . . ."

Folami recognized the voice as Abameta. He sounded panicked, something that didn't match his profile or her immediate impression of him at the briefing yesterday.

"Repeat, Abameta," Folami said, "you're breaking up."

Either the flight deck cleared some of the interference, or Abameta did on the ground. "We need backup—we're under attack."

"By who?"

"The missing Ori-Inu."

SIX
An unnamed ship

ORANMIYAN WRAPPED HIS ARMS AROUND Abeje, kissing her passionately, even as Abeje's parents dismissed her governess and a dozen Eso attacked her.

Shaking her head, Abeje tried to get her mind under control.

The memories were coming back in bits and pieces, and they confused and terrified Abeje.

Born on Oshun, a child of privilege. Sent into Ori-Inu training. Oranmiyan trained her, yet they were in bed together?

Did he take advantage of me?

No, that didn't make sense. Oranmiyan wouldn't do that to her.

He punched you in the face. He trapped you in a tube. He made you his prisoner.

No, he's making me free!

He faked his own death. He injected you with—with something. Shango-oti, he called it.

After that injection, when Abeje woke up, it wasn't in a darkened room or a claustrophobic tube, but a standard-issue cabin in a standard-issue transport. There was a desk, a bunk, and a commode. She woke up on the bunk, less concerned about where she was than *who* she was.

Oranmiyan came in and asked, "How're you feeling?"

"That—that is a very complicated question," she said honestly.

Unable to deal with what was inside her head, she projected outward, instead.

The ship had been on a parabolic orbit that took it back to Oshun after a day and a half. Abeje found that she was now able to hear so many thoughts she hadn't been able to hear before. One she recognized as Akanke, and she realized that the other Ori-Inu in the tubes had been awakened as well.

No, wait, she thought and concentrated. "I don't believe this—I can sense twenty other minds in the ship now. Sense them so perfectly clear. Oranmiyan, the sensation of a mind used to be a blip on a scanner, now—" She stared up at him. He was smiling broadly. "It's as if all twenty of them are *right here*, having a conversation with me." She shook her head. "It's like I've been color blind my whole life, and now I'm seeing a rainbow."

"That's the Shango-oti, sweets. It increases your telepathy, gives you all your memories back—it makes you free."

Abeje didn't know about that last part, but she couldn't argue with the first two. She could sense so much more, and so much more clearly, and her life from before Hembadoon recruited her was filtering back.

Oranmiyan calling her "sweets" still made her twitch, but for different reasons now. She regarded him with a heavy heart. "Why did you fake your death?"

The smile fell from Oranmiyan's face. "I had to, sweets. I couldn't stay in training anymore, not once I saw them for what they were. That super-soldier you, me, and Folami went up against? It changed me. But I couldn't just leave unless I made sure they didn't try to look for me."

A day ago, Abeje would not have believed such nonsense, but she remembered now that Oranmiyan had indeed been changed by that Oyo super-soldier. Ever since then, nobody could scan Oranmiyan, and apparently the changes went deeper than that. "All the mindwiping got reversed, didn't it?"

"More than that," Oranmiyan said. "I *can't* be mindwiped, sweets. I remembered *everything* they did to us."

Abeje was starting to remember that herself.

"I only came to Oshun to check on the project," Oranmiyan said, "but that little explosion that happened down there has changed things a bit."

Abeje blinked. "What explosion?"

"There was a spy from Oyo who was trying to sabotage the refinery. That's why I was there in the first place, to find him. You got to him first, is all—and I got to you, luckily. But I figured he was all done for after I zapped his brain." Oranmiyan shook his head. "The *buruku* went and blew up the refinery. Right now, there's a dozen Ori-Inu trying to find out what happened. We have to destroy *all* the evidence of Ojiji before they find it—*and* maybe get some new recruits."

"More Ori-Inu for the ranks?" Abeje asked.

"Not Ori-Inu. We are Nide—we are *free*."

One of the first things that Abameta learned in the field was that sometimes the best way to be invisible *wasn't* to use technology.

The armor's stealth mode had its uses, of course, but there were times when you just needed to gather information. And that meant you didn't need to be hidden in the traditional sense.

Sometimes you needed to infiltrate.

Putting the armor in stealth mode had several problems,

not the least of which was a huge consumption of power. It also meant you had to move in the shadows, not interact in any way with anyone or anything. And again, that had its uses.

But the mission here was as much to gather information as it was to fight, and right now the best place to do that was *not* in the shadows.

So Abameta abandoned his armor in favor of a cable-knit woolen sweater, work boots, and skintight wool pants—ordinary clothes for autumn in Kaduna Township, ones that would spare him from even a first look, much less a second one.

Scanning a dozen different natives had revealed to Abameta that the finest restaurant in the township was Odungan—which meant it would be the most crowded.

The place was located in a cul-de-sac. Unlike most of the buildings around it, the restaurant was made of brick. While less sturdy than the alloys that were used for construction, the red bricks and gray mortar gave the place a very subdued, pleasant atmosphere. The other places Abameta had seen on Oshun were functional—Odungan felt luxurious by comparison.

Upon entering, the server gave him an apologetic glance. "I'm sorry, but there's at least a one-hour wait." Without even trying, Abameta could feel her anxiety. The young woman had been reprimanded for being rude to a customer. She hadn't been, but the customer complained, and that got her in trouble. She was now paralyzed with fear at the notion of losing her job, which would happen if someone else complained about her.

Looking past her, Abameta could see that all the tables were occupied. He already knew that before he walked in thanks to his quick scan of the inside, but the server would expect him to do so.

She quickly added, "But if you wish, you may have a drink

at the bar until a table opens up."

Abameta nodded. "That'll be fine."

Relief washed over the server like a wave, and a bigger wave came when Abameta gave her a brief smile.

The bar was just as crowded as the restaurant was, but Abameta had little difficulty navigating through the crowds to a single stool that was available. He ordered a fruit juice, and immediately started a general scan of the vicinity.

However, the thoughts he received were even more boring than those of the middle-management types in the hospital.

But that was part of the job. You had to be patient. So he sorted through them. This one worrying about whether his job would be extended beyond the six months he was promised. Those two talking about the weather, wondering whether it would warm up before winter hit. Three more comparing notes on a music performance they'd just come back from. This one telling that one about her family and how she just needed to get away from them. Another wondering what was taking his meal so long. The server wishing she didn't have to work here, her feet just *killing* her.

"I want a table!"

Abameta looked up in surprise at the voice, because it didn't come with a concomitant set of thoughts. Looking over at the front entrance, he saw Akin, carrying his Bayo, wearing his full armor.

"I'm sorry, sir, but—" the server started nervously, but Akin interrupted.

"I'm an Ori-Inu, here on a priority mission. Either give me a table, or I shut this place down."

The server's anxiety went into overdrive, and she was now convinced that she'd be fired.

Akin would probably have done worse to her than that if he was angered.

"Can—can you just give me a minute, please? We'll get a table ready."

"Make it fast," Akin said. Abameta couldn't actually scan his fellow Ori-Inu, but he hardly needed to. Impatience radiated off of him.

Shaking his head, Abameta sipped his juice, fearing for what this would do to his surveillance. Sure enough, everyone saw the Ori-Inu battle suit, and they tightened up. Thoughts become more guarded as people grew more nervous.

Now I'm never going to find out anything. Stupid buruku.

Then, to make matters worse, Akin walked over to him. "Abameta?"

"What do you want?" Abameta asked, not even looking at his fellow Ori-Inu.

Now Akin was smiling brightly. "Some dinner, I'm starving. And after eating cavalry mush for weeks, I'm looking forward to some *real* food. Wanna join me?"

"No thanks. Just want to have a quiet drink."

"You sure? I hear this place has the best food on Oshun."

"I'm fine."

"Okay." Akin frowned. "Was kinda hoping for some company. Maybe we can compare notes, and—"

Finally, Abameta turned to look at Akin. He was young, of course—they were all young, to Abameta—and looked like a kicked puppy at Abameta's refusal to dine with him.

At Abameta's look, Akin visibly cringed, but he kept talking. "Look, you're practically a legend! I'd love a chance to—"

Turning his back on the boy, Abameta said, "Go eat your dinner."

The server's small voice sounded from behind them. "Uh, sir? Your, uh—your table's ready."

At that, Akin turned and followed her.

Stupid buruku, Abameta thought as he finished off his fruit juice and ordered another.

Abeje rolled the word around in her head: *Nide*.

She wasn't sure if she liked the sound of it.

But a new name was necessary, because no matter what, she simply could no longer consider herself an Ori-Inu. Thinking of herself as a tool of the Hegemony was no longer possible. Whatever else Shango-oti had done for her—to her—she couldn't let herself be Ori-Inu anymore.

Because she knew what the Hegemony really did. They didn't *just* mindwipe you at the end of your training. Abeje, Oranmiyan, Folami, and the others they trained with under Hembadoon were mindwiped *dozens* of times, sometimes for the most minor of infractions.

The Hegemony's party line that the mindwiping was due to wishing the Ori-Inu to be the finest possible warriors was, she now realized, a rationalization.

They mindwiped Ori-Inu to make them better slaves.

Abeje wasn't going to be anyone's slave anymore.

But she wasn't sure she wanted to be one of Oranmiyan's Nide either.

"Come on," Oranmiyan said, leading her out of the cabin and down a winding corridor. "We'll be in orbit soon."

"Won't they detect us?"

Shaking his head, Oranmiyan smiled. "We're fogging the orbital station's minds, and the folks down on the ground."

That shocked Abeje. "*All* of them?"

"Yup. They're seeing what we want them to see."

"Oranmiyan, that's crazy. Even *Folami* couldn't do that." Folami was tenth-level, and was one of most powerful psis known to exist.

"Told you Shango-oti was liberating, sweets. It's a new day, and the Ori-Inu aren't part of it. The future belongs to *us*."

They turned a corner and entered a small dropship bay. Abeje saw the remaining five Ori-Inu—or, rather, Nide—all dressed in white body armor. How much armor each person wore varied from person to person. Several had full armor including a featureless helmet with a tube connecting it to a back piece that presumably contained an air supply. Another tube, this one for ammunition, linked from that same back piece to a gun on the left glove. Others went for partials.

Abeje was still in her hospital gown, and now was self-conscious about it. She knew she was attractive, and as an Ori-Inu, she had used that to her advantage. Now, though, it felt odd to be flaunting that in front of these five new teammates.

Nobody seemed to care, though. That actually disappointed her.

Oranmiyan projected his thoughts to everyone in the bay. *Folks, this is our newest recruit, Abeje. She and I go back to our training days.*

One of the women removed her helmet, revealing the round face of Akanke, who spoke aloud. "Good to see you, Abeje, it's incredibly great to have you here, and I'm really really really glad that Oranmiyan brought you in!"

That gave Abeje pause. "Uh, thanks," she managed to blurt out, but Akanke's rapid-fire delivery was bizarre to say the least. Akanke had always been taciturn at best, laconic at worst, rarely using three words when one would do.

Oranmiyan led Abeje to a back room where there was a door with **abeje** inscribed on it. The door slid aside to reveal her armor.

While she changed, Oranmiyan went back out to the bay, and projected the mission profile to them all.

We got ten Ori-Inu dirtside on Oshun, with two more at Kaduna Orbital, and another one on L'owuro.

As she put on her armor, Abeje realized that she could feel *everyone* in the telepathic conversation. They'd done briefs like this before, both during training and afterward, but she'd only felt the person doing the briefing on those occasions. Now, though, she distinctly felt each and every one of the Nide.

Ayoola, you take care of Kaduna Orbital. The rest of us go dirtside. Bolade, you take out anyone connected to Ojiji who's still breathing. Foluke, you get whatever's left of the refinery. I don't even want there to be microscopic residue of the records of Ojiji's existence. Akanke, Sere, you two get the Ori-Inu.

Now Abeje found herself at the center of a standard scan—it was as if she was *inside* the scan. Oranmiyan had done this sort of thing back during training, but then he just projected an image of the scan in their heads. Now it was a part of her.

The scan was of Kaduna Township, with red dots indicating where each Ori-Inu was. Akanke and Sere now knew where each of the Ori-Inu on the surface were.

Abeje and I will be the backup in case things go wrong.

They turned and boarded the dropship. Abeje had, at this point, put on all the armor save for the helmet. To her surprise, the only weapons were the wrist-mounted rifle on her left gauntlet—of course Oranmiyan remembered that she was left-handed—and a titanium knife sheathed on her thigh.

Oranmiyan read her surprise as she came out from the back room. "You won't need too many weapons, sweets. See, when you're a Nide, you *are* the weapon."

Immediately, Abeje flashed on one of Hembadoon's many sayings: "As an Ori-Inu, you'll be a weapon—but you should always have a spare. With weapons, it's better to have more than you need than less than you need."

Before she could speak, though, Oranmiyan jumped in. "Yeah, I know what the Orisha said. And he was right—but being a Nide *is* more than you'll need. Trust me."

The dropship's main compartment had one long bench facing the side door, with shorter benches on either side of that door, a rear hatch, and another door to the cockpit. A civilian was piloting, with Bolade, Foluke, and Akanke on the long bench, and Sere on the right side of the door.

Oranmiyan and Abeje took the bench to the left of the door, which Oranmiyan shut behind him. "Let's go!"

As they waited for the bay to depressurize, Oranmiyan looked down at Abeje and smiled. She shuddered—she missed that smile, she realized.

"You haven't asked me yet," Oranmiyan finally said.

"Asked you what?"

"Why you're being held back."

"No, I understand that," Abeje said, to her own surprise. "I've just been—well, freed. Or whatever. I still don't know the full extent of my abilities, so it's better if I stay behind. But I *do* have a question."

"Yeah?"

"Why did you let me—let *us* think you were dead?"

Abeje still couldn't read Oranmiyan's mind, but his face spoke volumes just then.

"I had my reasons," was all he'd say out loud as he turned away.

"That's it? Me, Folami, Hembadoon—we thought you were *dead*! We had a memorial service and everything!"

"I couldn't stay there, Abeje. Not with what I knew." He looked back down at her. The sadness in his brown eyes had been replaced with anger. "The Hegemony is keeping telepaths down, and that can't happen anymore. We're the future, Abeje, and Isembi's been keeping us as slaves. But that stops now. Shango-oti's the key, sweets. We'll be on top of the galaxy, now!"

Abeje frowned. Oranmiyan was using slogans to cover an answer to her question. "If you needed to leave so badly that you had to fake your death—"

"It was the only way I could leave without Hembadoon coming after me. They had to think I was gone."

"Fine—so why wouldn't you take me with you?"

Now Oranmiyan's eyes were hard. "Because you wouldn't have come. You were a good little mindwiped Ori-Inu. You wouldn't have scanned me, sweets, you'd have turned me in, like a good little trainee."

Abeje wanted to object, but deep down, she knew he was right.

And then the dropship landed. Abeje barely noticed it.

One by one, the Nide disembarked, going in different directions.

Akanke *loved* the Shango-oti!

She was practically bouncing in her seat while she waited for the dropship to land on Oshun so she could start kicking some ass.

Akanke *loved* kicking ass.

Best of all, she'd be kicking Ori-Inu ass. Akanke hated Ori-Inu. That she'd been an Ori-Inu didn't matter, because she wasn't one anymore, and now that she was a Nide she knew how awful Ori-Inu were, so anybody who was still an Ori-Inu had to be awful and needed to be killed and *immediately* so that they stopped polluting the galaxy with their awfulness.

Her first assignment was the two Ori-Inu that were in a restaurant. Akanke had no idea where Oranmiyan got the codes for their neural implants, but Akanke didn't really care that much, she just knew that it meant that she'd be able to track Abameta and Akin right to where they were so she could kick their asses.

Akanke really liked the ass-kicking part.

It was so much better than when *she* was Ori-Inu. Then she was just some passive loser, wandering from mission to mission, not caring about anything.

Now, though, everything was about the ass-kicking. No more doing whatever Oba Isembi told her to do, oh no, not that, not anymore, she was her own woman now.

And now she was going to kick Akin and Abameta's asses.

Once the dropship landed, Akanke put her helmet back on. Abeje and Oranmiyan had been talking on and on and on about *some* nonsense or other, but now it was all ready to go and kick some ass time.

Akanke's favorite time.

As soon as the rear hatch opened, Akanke headed in the direction provided by her helmet's HUD, though the heads-up display was redundant, since she had the location in her so-much-more-powerful-now mind. Still, it was good to have confirmation—plus, the targets could move . . .

She ran through the streets, hiding her presence from the flatbrains around them. The idea was to surprise the Ori-Inu, and it would be hard to do that if the whole population of Kaduna started screaming about white-armored people running through the streets.

Luckily, blanking the flatbrains' minds to their presence was really really really really easy, thanks to Shango-oti. Akanke just *loved* Shango-oti.

Akanke checked the HUD again. To her surprise, Abameta was sitting at the restaurant's bar, while Akin was seated in a booth on the far end of the place. From orbit, they hadn't been able to pinpoint it that precisely.

She wondered why they weren't eating together for only a moment before she remembered that she didn't care.

She was Nide now. She did things her own way.

I'm gonna take you, Ori-Inu.

Abameta sat up straight in his bar stool.

The telepathic "voice" didn't sound like any of the Ori-Inu currently at Oshun. What was—?

The west wall of Odungan caved in suddenly, the crumbling brick shattering the subdued sussurus of the restaurant.

Standing on the other side of the new hole in the wall was a figure in white armor. Abameta felt Akin project at him: *How did we not sense this coming?*

However, it was the white-armored woman who replied. *Because I didn't want you to, Ori-Inu!*

The panicked customers all ran toward the exits—or toward windows, anything that would get them away. Abameta could sense that some were injured under the rubble that the crazy woman had created.

Then all the people in the restaurant ceased screaming, ceased moving, and fell to the floor, blood coming from their noses and ears.

This is really bad, Abameta thought. He didn't have his weapons with him—this was supposed to be surveillance—and she had already mindblasted everyone in the restaurant. Abameta felt them all dying at once, all wondering who the strange person in white armor was.

Abameta, though, knew who she was, because she was in the files that Folami had provided: Akanke, one of the Ori-Inu who'd gone missing, and whose disappearances that Orisha had been investigating when the refinery blew up.

What is she doing here?

Akanke's voice sounded in his head. *Killing you.*

She aimed her wrist cannon right at Abameta's chest, but Abameta was able to dive behind the bar.

Mogbe, *those are rifle rounds,* Abameta thought as he looked quickly around, sighting a whiskey bottle in the grip of the dead bartender's hand. He could hear the reports of Akin's Bayo and Akanke's wrist rifle across the restaurant, and Abameta had a feeling that his fellow Ori-Inu was going to come out on the wrong end of that one.

Sure enough, Akin screamed a moment later.

Akanke then stuck her head over the bar. "It's all over, old man." She aimed her wrist cannon at Abameta.

Abameta said, "I've heard that before."

He grabbed the bottle from the bartender's hand and shoved it, bottom-first, into the barrel of the wrist cannon, then ducked under the bartender's corpse.

The rifle round smashed into the glass of the bottle, igniting the alcohol inside, and retarding the round's momentum before it could clear the barrel. Akanke screamed in agony as her forearm was shredded by the blast.

Shrapnel flew through the air, much of it slicing into the

bartender—who was beyond feeling it—and into Abameta's left leg—which wasn't. But he ignored the pain, wishing he had his body armor with its supply of painkillers.

It would only take Akanke a few seconds to recover, and Abameta needed to use those seconds to report this in. As he pulled out his comm unit, he sensed other attacks happening elsewhere in Kaduna. *This is really really bad.*

Once he activated the unit, he barked, "This is an emergency. We need backup immediately to assist against hostiles."

"Repeat, Abameta, you're breaking up."

Abameta snarled. "We need backup—we're under attack."

"By who?"

"The missing Ori-Inu. Aaaaarrrrrrrrrrhhhhhhhh!"

Akanke was now trying to fry his brain. But Abameta had known Akanke back in the day, and he knew that she was only a fifth-level—the minimum required for being a proper telepath.

So Abameta struck back.

Or tried to. As a sixth-level, Abameta should have had the upper hand, but instead he was barely able to hold his own. They were locked together.

Nice try, but I'm much stronger than your old ass now.

Abameta grimaced. *Stronger than you were, maybe. You used to use your brains to compensate. You never would've fallen for that trick with the whiskey bottle in the old days, Akanke. What happened?*

You want to know what happened? Shango-oti freed me, old man, that's what happened!

Suddenly, Abameta realized that this wasn't just a hit on Ori-Inu. Shango-oti was what Ojiji was developing. Apparently, it was already in use supercharging Ori-Inu.

Abameta's first thoughts were to his duty as an Ori-Inu. *I have to live long enough to report this.*

That is not happening, old man! You're already dead, you just haven't stopped breathing yet.

Abameta knew better. Normally, he'd be right, but Akanke's injuries were starting to get the better of her. Her right arm was a useless stump, and her attention was split between shutting off her pain receptors and fighting Abameta.

Even so, it took everything Abameta had to try to push through Akanke's shields, even temporarily, trying to sense what Akanke was trying to hide . . .

. . . returning from a mission, the ship coming under attack . . .

. . . being boarded by Ori-Inu in strange white armor . . .

. . . meeting Oranmiyan and being given a chance for freedom . . .

. . . fighting Oranmiyan and losing . . .

. . . waking up with her neural implant gone and her telepathy increased . . .

. . . becoming a Nide.

It's over, Akanke, Abameta said. *I'm going to beat you.*

No chance. Akanke's smile widened.

Abameta felt his own shields start to crumble. *This makes no sense, she's just a fifth-level—*

And then he realized what it was he'd read in her thoughts. She wasn't fifth-level, not anymore.

Abameta tried to call for help, but all his focus had to be on maintaining his own psychic shields against Akanke's increasingly nasty onslaught until someone—anyone—could come to his aid.

His last thoughts before Akanke's mindblasted him were regret that he wouldn't be able to give a final report.

SEVEN
Oshun

BY THE TIME FOLAMI LANDED on Oshun, all the other Ori-Inu were dead. She'd felt them die in her mind.

Just all those people in Nupe . . .

Mogbe!

It was another memory, clear as a holograph, fleeting as a breath. Folami was used to feeling people die—it was part of life as a tenth-level—but these were her comrades. What was worse was that most of them were killed without all that much of a fight.

Two of them didn't even have the chance to try to fight—the pair she'd sent to the orbital station were destroyed when a ship came out of nowhere and blew the station to atoms. Tobi had tried to retaliate, but *L'owuro's* scanners couldn't get a fix on the ship that did the deed.

She was going down to the surface now with a contingent from Rufiji Company, originally with the notion of backing up the Ori-Inu, but by the time the dropship landed, it had become revenge.

So be it. I beat the Eso, I'll beat these people. She tried not to think about how, precisely, she was supposed to beat an unknown number of ex-Ori-Inu, who apparently had been hyped up on this Shango-oti stuff, based on how easily they took out their former comrades.

Updates were coming in from *L'owuro*. "The refinery's been completely leveled. Whatever was left intact after the explosion is gone now. Reports are coming in of strange people in white armor appearing out of nowhere."

Folami turned to Cavalry Master Apara, who'd been promoted to replace Fasina, something that Cavalry Master Morayo resented. "Abameta said that these were the missing Ori-Inu. They must have some of the same stealth tech."

Apara just shrugged. She wasn't one to speak overmuch, which Folami suspected was why Tobi had promoted her over the more outspoken Morayo. The war chief generally preferred to be the only outspoken person in the room.

The dropship put down smoothly just outside where the refinery used to be.

When Folami stepped out, the stench nearly made her fall over. The stink of burning metal mixed with the overwhelming odor of spilled blood.

Dead bodies were strewn amid the rubble. A quick glance was enough to make Folami realize why there was so much blood: it was oozing out of their eyes and noses and ears.

Which meant that they were mindblasted.

A sufficiently powerful psi could simply fry someone's brain, and this was the result. But Folami had never seen anything on this scale before.

Yes, you have! In Nupe.

Another recollection, this of a stadium full of people, hundreds of them . . .

Killed by me. For Olorun's sport.

Then, just as quickly, the memory was gone.

Fighting down the nausea, both at the stench here on Oshun and the awful realization that she'd been responsible for something similar in the past, Folami managed to move out and allow the rest of Rufiji Company to fall in.

Whoever did this, Folami decided, *is going to pay.*

Then she felt it.

"We're not alone," she told Apara. "There's a telepath heading right for us."

Apara checked the scanner in her helmet. "I'm not picking anything up."

"Oh, she's good," Folami said, a frown forming on her face. "But she's here." She closed her eyes a moment, and concentrated, showing Apara what she sensed.

"Whoa!" Apara stumbled for a second, her armor keeping her upright.

This telepath had placed a psionic perceptual filter in the heads of Apara and the other members of Rufiji. *No wonder the other Ori-Inu didn't stand a chance,* Folami thought.

All of a sudden, the woman became visible. Folami could sense some of her surface thoughts. She called herself "Nide," the next generation of Ori-Inu.

More to the point, this was Foluke, one of the Ori-Inu that had been reported missing.

But there was more—her thoughts were hyped up, random, more active.

Stronger.

And she had committed murder a dozen times over. Tasked with destroying all evidence of Ojiji, she had gone further and casually killed anyone who happened to be in the area: relief workers trying to retrieve the bodies of those killed in the explosion, doctors and medics and nurses tending to the injured, engineers and construction workers trying to determine how the place could be rebuilt.

All dead at the hands of this so-called Nide.

Ori-Inu existed to protect the Hegemony and its citizenry. Nide perverted all of that. Folami's nausea now was even worse—and so was her anger.

Conveniently, she even had a target for it.

Foluke spoke. "It's over, Folami. We already took care of the others. We don't want to have to take care of you, as well."

Folami smiled. "Oh, you won't be."

Clenching her fists, Folami reached out with her mind and tore through Foluke's armor, ripping through its circuitry.

Even as her armor sparked and burned and shorted out, Folami aimed her Bayo and blasted a hole in her chest.

Rufiji Company hadn't even had a chance to react before Folami killed the Nide. Apara slowly said, "Uh, that—that was—well, impressive. Woulda been nice to have one to question, though."

"They're called Nide. They're what Ojiji appears to be about. They've all been exposed to the same Shango-oti gas that was released by the refinery explosion."

"Very good, Folami. You're still the best."

Folami whirled around toward the source of the voice. Somehow, one of the Nide had managed to sneak up on all of them without her sensing it.

Prepared for another fight, she felt her stomach flutter when she realized that she recognized the person who had spoke.

"Oranmiyan? But—but you're dead!"

"Interesting." Oranmiyan seemed surprised. "You remember me?"

Memories leapt to the fore, then disappeared. Training

missions, meals shared, classes . . . "I— Yes, we—didn't we train together?"

"That's right, Folami."

She forcefully tamped down the memories. "You're responsible for this massacre, aren't you?"

"There's a lot more going on here, Folami. Why don't you come back with me to Olokun Station? Abeje'll be there, too."

More memories—no, the same ones. Abeje and Oranmiyan and Folami, all training with Hembadoon.

"You took Abeje?" Folami raised her Bayo. "What is going on here, Oranmiyan? I want answers, now!"

But Oranmiyan just smiled and turned and ran into the streets of Kaduna Township. Folami—who was used to using her telepathy to aid in targeting—was frustrated by her inability to get a fix on Oranmiyan.

Another memory: Oranmiyan mindlinking with an Oyo super-soldier, and unable to be read by any telepaths after that, not even Folami.

But the clearest memory she had of Oranmiyan was his dying. She even remembered his memorial.

Snarling, she chased after him, ignoring the pleas of Cavalry Master Apara.

The streets of Kaduna Township were covered in corpses and damaged buildings, whether by the Eso, the explosion, or the Nide. Seeing the carnage, the destruction, only lent urgency to Folami's task as she ran through the streets.

But she didn't see the bodies of the citizens of Kaduna. No, she saw Olorun, the self-styled God of the Oyo Empire, who had groomed Folami as his greatest weapon. She saw the prisoners of the state arrayed in the soccer stadium, lined up for Folami to mindblast at his command. She saw Olorun's chamberlain try to recruit her to his coup, instead dying at her hands for his treason. She saw a mineshaft destroyed by her telekinesis, supposedly the secret headquarters of the chamberlain's allies, but only filled with innocent miners, dead at her hands.

She saw Hembadoon, who risked his life to infiltrate enemy territory and rescue her from Yemoja.

Her one condition on accepting the Orisha's offer to become an Ori-Inu for the Hegemony—the Oyo Empire's blood enemy—was a guarantee that she'd be mindwiped at the end of it so she'd never have to remember the deaths.

And now she was remembering them all over again.

There was something else, something she couldn't quite grasp, something that happened at the end of her training, but it stayed just out of her mental reach. She wasn't even sure she wanted to know what it was, given what else she remembered.

I'm going to catch up to you, Oranmiyan.

Gotta find me first, sweets.

Folami snarled again. Now he was simply taunting her by projecting his thoughts.

And she was sick of it.

She reached out with her mind and ripped apart the building nearest to her. If Oranmiyan was running along the rooftop, or using it to hide behind, she would expose him.

Brick, mortar, adobe, and metal shattered and twisted, screaming into the night as Folami's mind ripped the structures to pieces, hoping to expose Oranmiyan.

But he wasn't there.

At least, not physically. She couldn't find him with her eyes or her mind, but he was still continuing to taunt her telepathically. *You don't understand, sweets, Shango-oti will free you.*

Screaming, she tore another building to rubble. *Free me to do what?* she thought back at him. *To remember? I already remember more than I ever wanted to thanks to just a little bit of Shango-oti. Or maybe you mean I'll be free to commit mass murder?*

Means to an end, sweets.

I'm taking you down, you filthy buruku!

She pumped her legs through the devastated streets, tossing ground vehicles aside, blowing out windows and searching desperately for some kind of sign of Oranmiyan.

Then she cursed herself for forgetting her training—

. . . the training I did with Oranmiyan . . .

—and she activated the HUD in her suit. She and Oranmiyan had to be the only two people running through the city streets right now, beyond official vehicles like ambulances and enforcement—the few she hadn't destroyed, anyhow—and she could screen those from the search.

That scan revealed that Oranmiyan was right over her head.

Stopping, she looked up to see Oranmiyan crouching on the roof of one of the few buildings left intact. "About time you noticed, sweets."

"Don't call me that! Do you know what you've done?"

"We've been doing a lot more than that, Folami. And you can be part of it. Come with me—be free!"

"Free? You can't be serious," she said, keeping her weapon lowered. Oranmiyan was too fast for her to get a bead on him, and the roof had a cornice that ran deep and out of her line of fire.

"I'm completely serious, sweets. It's true—and I'll prove it to you! Now or later, it's your choice."

"Try never."

Then she concentrated and shattered the cornice. Hoping it would startle Oranmiyan, instead, he leapt backward just as it happened, doing a perfect backflip. His dreadlocks flipping behind him, he landed neatly on his feet, aiming his Ayoka at her face.

"Nice try, sweets, but we trained together, remember? Your nose always wrinkles when you're about to use the telekinesis."

He fired the weapon.

Folami was able to dodge the round by diving to the side, telekinetically moving herself and the bullet both. The round shattered a piece of rubble that was right behind her.

By the time she got to her feet, only a second later, Oranmiyan was gone.

This time, the HUD was useless. All she was able to read was herself, and the official vehicles. Oranmiyan might have been in one of those, but she had no way to know. She could have torn apart more buildings, but he'd revealed her tell. All she'd accomplish was to add to the considerable property damage in Kaduna Township.

Folami's brain was on automatic, her training making her act. She put a bulletin out on the Oshun Enforcement Net and to *L'owuro* to seek and locate Oranmiyan.

But even as she did that, she knew it was a lost cause.

She leaned her head back and yelled to the heavens at the top of her lungs, her mind tearing apart all the buildings nearby, shattering with cracks of destroyed matter that matched her primal scream.

EIGHT
L'owuro

THE FIRST THING HEMBADOON DID after he regained consciousness was sit up and stare at the scraggly faced young man in scrubs who entered the room. Based on the look of the place, the lack of windows, and his mild case of nausea, he figured he was in the infirmary of a spaceship, probably cavalry.

He asked the scraggly young man, "Where am I?"

The doctor stared at him in confusion. "I'm sorry?"

"It's a simple question, Doctor—you *are* a doctor, right?"

"Uh, yes—yes, I'm still Doctor Modupe, like I was when you woke up before. Orisha, I need you to lie back down and—"

Hembadoon did not lie back down. "Where am I?"

"You're still on the Hegemony Cavalry ship *L'owuro*. Now, p-please lie back down?"

The Orisha did so. *L'owuro* was War Chief Tobi's ship. Hembadoon had never liked Tobi, but he was grateful that Isembi had, at least, sent someone in after him when his mission went south.

Modupe then ran a slew of tests on Hembadoon, which the Orisha took in stride. When they were done, the doctor released him with the proviso that he check in every morning and that the medical scanner in his robes be tied into the infirmary, both of which were conditions Hembadoon was more than happy to abide by.

As soon as he left, he had his robe's computer bring him up to speed.

He wasn't sure what stunned him more, that the Eso had come and gone while he was out, that there was a top-secret project that even Isembi didn't know about on Oshun, or that Folami was here and in charge of the investigation.

She was also the last Ori-Inu standing, which somehow didn't surprise him. Hembadoon had been following Folami's career after her last mission as a trainee—that horrible, horrible day—and it had been an impressive string of successes, including several missions where she had been the only Ori-Inu to survive.

There was one other thing waiting for him. He had his suit interface with *Ebun*—which was currently in the dropship bay of *L'owuro* being repaired by a team of ship's engineers— and found that the computer had survived the explosion and the Eso attack. More to the point, it had finished running the program he'd started.

Hembadoon then made a beeline for War Chief Tobi's quarters, having his robe computer inform the war chief that he was on his way. If Tobi wasn't in his quarters, he would be there by the time Hembadoon arrived.

But Tobi wasn't there. Hembadoon waited, debating the efficacy of breaking the privacy seal on his door, then decided that was overstepping his authority.

A headache started to come on, which meant there was a telepath nearby. Since the only one left, according to the reports he'd read, was Folami . . .

Sure enough, he turned to see his former prize pupil. To

his utter shock, she was talking and laughing with a cavalry chief—a pilot, based on his haircut. Talking he could see, but in all his time as a Orisha, he had never seen an Ori-Inu interact with a flatbrain in so friendly a manner before. Ori-Inu generally kept to themselves, as only fellow telepaths really understood what they went through. Cavalry had a tendency to be afraid of Ori-Inu and often expressed their fear through hostility.

Folami looked up as soon as she turned the corner. "Orisha! You're awake!"

"Yup." Hembadoon stepped forward as if to embrace her, then stopped himself. Of course, Folami had no idea who he was beyond an unconscious body they found on Oshun after she stopped the Eso. "I, uh, I have to meet—uh, meet with War Chief Tobi." He shot a look at the cavalry chief, who was staring only at Folami, which angered Hembadoon more than was probably rational.

"About the Nide?"

"Huh?" Hembadoon shook his head. Talking business, he felt on firmer ground. "Uhm, I believe I know where this Olokun Station might be."

"Good." She sighed. "Because wherever Oranmiyan and the rest of them went, we can't trace them. They can trick anybody using a scanner so they don't see the actual readings, then make them wipe the scans. By the time I was able to get to them, they were gone."

"They can't do that to you?" the pilot asked.

"No. At least, not anymore. I broke through it on the surface. Oh!" She looked at the pilot, then Hembadoon. "Sorry, I'm forgetting my manners. Cavalry Chief Adejola, this is Orisha Hembadoon. Adejola's the Eta-shift pilot, and Hembadoon's the Orisha who recruited me."

That brought Hembadoon up short. "Hold on—you actually *remember* me?"

Folami nodded. "Side effect of Shango-oti."

"*Mogbe.*" Hembadoon wondered if it was better or worse that he didn't embrace her. Remembering the desperation with which Folami had asked for reassurance that she'd be mindwiped when her training ended, not to mention the reason for it, the Orisha added, "I'm sorry, Folami. I know you—"

"I know," she said quickly, "but there's nothing to be done about it right now. We've got to finish the mission, which means finding out where Oranmiyan and the other Nide went. If you've found Olokun—"

"I *think* I have. That's what I need to talk to the war chief about."

"I'll join you for that, if it's okay," Folami said in a tone that made it clear that it would have to be okay. "The Oba put me in charge of the investigation."

"Of course." Hembadoon only hadn't requested her presence because he wasn't sure if it was his place to do so.

"Well," Adejola said, clapping his hands to break the awkward pause that was starting to grow, "I guess dinner's off, then."

"Yes, Adejola," Folami said, "I'm sorry. I promise to make it up to you."

And why does this pilot get under my skin so much?

"Good to meet you, Orisha," Adejola said as he wandered off.

Hembadoon stared in confusion at Folami, but waited until the pilot was out of earshot before asking, "What's that about? Dinner?"

Folami shrugged, and smiled shyly, a smile he'd never seen her use before. "He likes me—as me, not as an Ori-Inu or as an object of desire. At least, he was interested in the person I was. Tonight was going to be the first time we talked since I got more of my memories back." The smile fell, and her entire body shuddered. "It's been horrible, Hembadoon. I remember so much . . ."

Instinctively, Hembadoon moved to put an arm around her, but before he could do so, a loud voice came from down the corridor.

"Orisha, I don't appreciate being yanked out of the flight deck by a—"

Folami interrupted before the Orisha could. "Orisha Hembadoon has some information that may help us to pinpoint the Nide, War Chief."

"Really?"

Hembadoon got his first good look at Tobi, and was less than impressed. Mostly his loud voice served to exacerbate the headache that being in Folami's presence gave him. Normally, he'd use the analgesics that his robe could pump right into his blood, but he was already on painkillers prescribed by Modupe. The analgesic wouldn't even register.

"Yes, really," Hembadoon said.

Tobi glared at Hembadoon, then at Folami, before finally approaching his cabin door, which slid aside once it registered the war chief's biometrics.

While the war chief took a seat at his desk, Hembadoon admired the various weapons that decorated the walls. "Impressive collection, War Chief."

"You a connoisseur of weaponry, Orisha?" Tobi asked, eyebrow raised.

"Not especially, I'm merely impressed by anyone who can gather that much of the same thing at once. The only items I was ever able to collect in such quantity were empty bottles of wine."

Now Tobi scowled. "Somehow I'm not surprised." He settled into his seat, arms folded over his barrel chest. "Now, would you mind explaining what's so important it was worth me ending a staff meeting prematurely?"

Folami smiled. "I thought you hated staff meetings, War Chief."

Hembadoon found himself smiling as well, and wondered if Folami had always been this irreverent with her military escorts, or if it was the memory of the aristocrat she used to be coming to the fore. Somehow, he couldn't imagine her tweaking, say, War Chief Titilayo like this.

Turning his scowl on Folami, Tobi said, "That isn't the point. We took a lot of casualties against the Eso, and there's been some rearrangement of personnel. Cleaning up after these Nide has just added to the difficulties."

Something nagged at Hembadoon in the way Tobi phrased that. "Hang on—casualties against the *Eso*?"

"Yes, Orisha," Tobi said in a slow, deliberate tone that one would use with a child, "we faced a battalion of Eso on Oshun. They killed a lot of my best people, including my XO, Cavalry Master Fasina."

"That's not what I meant," Hembadoon said impatiently. "I know about the Eso. What I'm curious about is that you didn't suffer any casualties at the hands of the Nide—considering that the number of people they killed on Oshun numbered in the hundreds, in addition to a dozen Ori-Inu."

Folami answered that. "Rufiji only faced one Nide, and

I took care of her. The rest escaped before any of us had the chance to do anything."

"And you couldn't find the ship they were using?" Hembadoon asked.

"They were blocking us," Tobi said.

"Wait a minute," Folami said, "don't your people have psi-screens?"

Tobi was getting testier by the minute. "What is this, a board of inquiry? Of *course* we have psi-screens, and we *used* them, but our scanners can't cover everything in orbit. That's what the orbital station's for, but—"

Folami winced. "But the Nide destroyed that, too."

"So if you're done crawling up my ass, would you mind telling me this brilliant idea of yours, Orisha, so I can get back to my real duties?"

Now Folami sounded like every bit the aristocrat she was born to be. "War Chief, this mission is the top priority of this vessel, as dictated to us by the Oba in this very room. This *is* your real duty."

"Fine, then let's get on with it."

Hembadoon watched the two of them stare each other down, wondering what the dynamic actually was here. Every time he thought he had a handle on it, he realized it was more complicated. Instinctively, he wanted to take Folami's side, but he wasn't even sure that Tobi was in the wrong in anything he did. Besides, it wasn't unusual for the cavalry support for Ori-Inu to resent their roles—that was why Adejola's being so ridiculously friendly with Folami was so bizarre in the first place.

Then he shrugged it off. *This isn't your problem, and Folami can take care of herself.*

He looked over at her, even more beautiful than she had been back when he recruited her. She had blossomed as an Ori-Inu.

Shaking it off, he subvocalized instructions to his robe computer to interface with the projector on Tobi's desk. "When I was looking into Abeje's disappearance, I came across several references to Olokun Station—including one made by her target, Kosoko, before he died in custody right before the refinery explosion. Now—"

Hembadoon cut himself off when he realized that Tobi was laughing. "You've got to be kidding me. Olokun Station? That's a fairy tale, Orisha. The awful place where bad Ori-Inu are taken to be punished. It's nonsense."

"And yet, it kept coming up in every investigation made into the missing Ori-Inu, up to and including this one."

"What, some madman in a cell mentions it and—"

Folami jumped in. "It's not just Kosoko. Oranmiyan mentioned Olokun, too. He wanted to take me there so his Shango-oti could 'free' me."

"I'm telling you," Tobi said, "it's a myth, and this is a waste of my time."

"Not so fast, War Chief," Hembadoon said, calling up a map of the system on Tobi's holograph. Then several red dots appeared at various points. "Each of those dots represents a place where there were mentions of Olokun Station in relation to a disappearing Ori-Inu."

Tobi raised an eyebrow. "So?"

Hembadoon could see that Folami had figured it out—or just read it in the Orisha's mind. "What's the order of the sightings?"

"Funny you should ask." Hembadoon subvocalized an instruction to his computer to draw a line through the various red dots in the order of the date of the reference.

The result was a more-or-less straight line from one dot to another in sequence.

"This is a course with no deviations," Hembadoon said. "Olokun Station is mobile."

Folami couldn't sleep.

Every time she closed her eyes, she saw the legions of the dead, strewn all across the streets of Kaduna Township.

But they were all the bodies from Nupe, the people she killed at Olorun's orders in the stadium, the miners she buried alive, and so many more. She remembered every single detail of every single person's mind.

It was precisely this that she became an Ori-Inu to forget.

And now so much had come back, thanks to Oranmiyan, someone she had thought was her friend.

Her memories of her training with Hembadoon had come back as well. Those, at least, she recalled with great fondness. Oranmiyan, Abeje, and Folami had formed a deep bond over many a session.

Of course she also recalled his death, and the devastation she and Abeje and Hembadoon had felt. Oranmiyan had been older than the other trainees, including Folami, and he had taken on the role of elder statesman, always giving friendly advice and encouragement.

And always with a smile. *That* was what was missing from Oranmiyan now. His warm, friendly smile.

But then, did she really *want* him to smile when he was responsible for so many deaths?

Folami stared at the ceiling of her cabin on *L'owuro*.

This, she thought as she got up from her bunk, *is getting me nowhere.*

Currently, *L'owuro* was conducting a thorough scan of the entire vicinity of Oshun—starting with Shango, the gas giant Oshun orbited, and moving ever outward, trying to find Olokun Station.

Unfortunately, that search could take weeks, especially since they had no idea what they were looking for, though Tobi was going on the logical assumption that it was disguised as an asteroid of some sort. Since Yemoja's destruction, there were bits of rock all over the place, so it would make a good disguise.

It was equally likely that, with the mission on Oshun completed, the Nide had moved on. Tobi had placed the entire area on lockdown, with psi-screen-enhanced techs staffing the scanners that would detect *any* unauthorized vessel. But Olokun could have slipped out before that net was cast.

Either way, they were at the most uninteresting part of any mission: waiting.

Normally, Folami would take advantage of the downtime to sleep. She'd been going strong for days now, with comparatively little rest. And she suspected that once they found Olokun, she would be in for the fight of her life. Oranmiyan trained with her. And, thanks to the haze of Shango-oti and mindwiping, he probably remembered her fighting style with greater clarity than she could. After all, there were still gaps in her memory. She recalled little of her life before Olorun recruited her, nor could she bring to mind what Hembadoon had called her "final exam" when she was officially made an Ori-Inu.

Closing her eyes just brought up mental images that would not be conducive to sleep.

During their training, Hembadoon had always said, "Always go in with at least two plans, because in any engagement, you're guaranteed to need both of them."

Folami's body armor hung next to her bed for easy access. She slept in her underclothing, ready to suit up at a moment's notice. She slipped out of bed and padded over to the commode, where she found a silk bathrobe with the Hegemony Cavalry logo on the pockets, and matching slippers. Though tall for her sex, Folami was apparently shorter than the average cavalry. The standard-issue robe only came down to her calves.

In fact, the robe was rather tight around the chest, which made Folami wonder who was supposed to have this cabin; it wasn't as though there weren't female cavalry . . .

Shrugging, she left her cabin and made a right down the corridor.

Tobi had called General Quarters, so she didn't encounter anybody in the corridor. Technically, she was violating GQ by doing what she was doing, but technically, she wasn't part of L'owuro's chain of command, so she wasn't obligated to follow Tobi's orders.

She approached Adejola's door. At her approach, the camera outside the door showed him inside who was on the other side. At a word from him, the door slid aside to reveal that the pilot had begun to change out of his uniform. His chest was bare, and Folami couldn't help but notice the quality of his muscle tone. Then again, she knew he took pride in his workout regimen. Over dinner, he had talked about how he hated being sedentary and that the one thing he disliked about piloting was having to sit around for so long.

"Uh, hi, Folami. Is something wrong?"

"Actually, yes," she said honestly. "I can't sleep, and I could use your help."

Adejola frowned. "Well, you'd be better off seeing the doctor, I can't—"

"Not medical help—exactly. May I come in?"

"Uh, sure, sure."

Folami smiled as he stepped aside to allow her ingress. She couldn't read any specific surface thoughts, though her impression was one of nervousness. He also stared at the V-neck formed by the robe.

"So how am I supposed to provide this not-really-medical help?" Adejola asked as he walked over to a sideboard where he kept a clear bottle filled with a green liquid.

Sitting down at the foot of his bunk, Folami said, "I need a distraction. Ever since we got here, the mindwipe they did to me after I was done with my training has been coming undone."

"I didn't know that was possible."

Folami nodded. "It's difficult, but not impossible. You can't really eliminate memories without removing brain tissue, and that's too risky. What mindwiping does is block access to those memories."

"And you've been able to re-access them?" Adejola frowned and held up the bottle. "Drink?"

"No, thanks." Folami had tried the green liquid—the drink was called a highmaker, though some called it a grenade due to its effect—and had no desire to have it again. Alcohol and telepathy wasn't the best mix in any case.

Pouring himself a glass, Adejola asked, "What do you remember?"

"Horrible things." Folami shuddered. "Things I *want* to forget."

He put a comforting hand on her thigh. "Then forget them. There must be *some* good memories."

She looked down at the hand. His concern was genuine,

although she could feel that he was still very nervous. Even through the silk, his touch was almost electric. She felt a shiver of desire.

"I've tried," she said, "but even the good ones lead to bad ones. I think about my parents—but then I think about how they turned me over to a tyrant. I think about my friends growing up—but they're dead. I think about my training, but then I think about Oranmiyan and Abeje—Oranmiyan is ringleading the Nide, and I'm pretty sure Abeje's been recruited by them, too."

Folami had never had a proper sexual encounter in her life. She'd certainly had plenty of offers, in Nupe, during training, and since becoming an Ori-Inu, but she'd always turned them down. Before her parents simply gave her to Olorun, she was saving herself for the right boy. While servicing the Oyo Empire, such things were not permitted. And during her training, all that mattered was achieving her goal of becoming an Ori-Inu.

And since then, there were only her missions.

But now, she felt only desire for this man with his nervous smile, who had been one of only two people who had shown her kindness and not betrayed it later. And seeing him here with his shirt off, she wanted nothing more than to let herself be wrapped in his well-muscled arms.

And maybe, if she lost herself in his arms, she could forget all those who died at her hands.

"Oranmiyan once told me that telepathic sex was a thousand times better than it was for flatbrains," she said suddenly.

Choking on his drink, Adejola managed to swallow and say, "Really?"

Just as quickly, she put a hand to her mouth. "Oh *mogbe*—

I'm sorry, I can't believe I said that."

He leaned close to her. She could smell the highmaker on his breath. He whispered, "I'm not sorry."

The kiss they shared made the touch on her leg feel inconsequential. Their tongues danced around each other, and their lips came hungrily together, and she wrapped her arms around him and suddenly there was nothing but him.

It was the most blissful feeling Folami had ever experienced.

The kiss went on forever. It ended too soon.

Adejola got to his feet. "I need to use the commode." Somehow, Folami's silk robe had come undone and lay open. Adejola stared appreciatively at her body before dashing toward the door. He turned around, and held up both hands. "*Please* don't go anywhere."

"I won't," she whispered.

He smiled. "Good."

The door shut behind him, and Folami slipped out of the robe. She left her underclothes on for the moment, thinking that Adejola might enjoy the act of undressing her himself. She almost wished she had worn more clothes—but all she had was her armor, and that was hardly appropriate.

Folami's heart was pounding hard against her rib cage. She couldn't believe she was doing this, but she also wanted it desperately. Her emotions were churning in her gut and she needed some kind of release.

She tried to force herself to calm down, using the breathing techniques Hembadoon had taught her. It wouldn't do to be too eager, after all.

But she was having trouble breathing.

The room started to swim about and blur. *What's going on?*

She tried to get to her feet, but her legs were like rubber, and she collapsed to the deck.

"Ad—Adejola?"

Her voice was a cracked whisper. She tried to raise her arm, but couldn't.

Then darkness took her.

NINE
Olokun Station

ORANMIYAN CALLED A MEETING OF all the surviving Nide in the wardroom.

He was, to say the least, extremely angry.

Abeje had gone in with him, asking what was wrong, but Oranmiyan wouldn't say anything about that, so she tried a different tack.

"That was Folami you saw on Oshun, wasn't it?"

At that, Oranmiyan softened. "Yeah. When you disappeared, they assigned an Orisha to investigate. When the refinery blew up, they sent her."

She chuckled. "It's like a reunion. We have to get her to join up, too, Oranmiyan! It'll be like old times."

Oranmiyan shook his head. "She didn't sound all that interested."

"Maybe I can talk to her."

They arrived at the wardroom. "Maybe."

As soon as they entered, Oranmiyan's stone face came back.

Abeje sat in one of the chairs around a big wooden table. Oranmiyan started pacing in a circle around the table. Suddenly, she was glad she couldn't read him—she doubted that his mind was a pleasant place to look into right now.

"You mind telling me what that was about on Oshun, people?"

Akanke bristled—Abeje could feel it as if it was she herself feeling the emotion—and said, "We were doing what you *told* us to do, Oranmiyan! Stop the Ori-Inu, wipe Ojiji, get out." She gestured with her left arm, her damaged right immobilized in a cast.

"There was *nothing* about killing flatbrains in there."

Sere laughed. "You're fogging us, right, Oranmiyan? Who gives a damn about flatbrains? They're just in the way."

Oranmiyan pointed at Sere. "That is *not* what we're about."

Abeje didn't like the way this was going. "Aren't civilian casualties a necessary evil?"

Glaring at her, Oranmiyan said, "Yeah, sometimes you get collateral damage, but that's not what I'm talking about."

He activated the holograph, which revealed a feed from a traffic monitor. It showed Akanke entering the restaurant where the Ori-Inu she was assigned to were both eating.

Abeje watched as they fought—and as the Nide lashed out at the civilians who were panicking and running away from them. They were all lying dead on the floor moments later.

Fighting down nausea, Abeje continued to observe as Oranmiyan switched the image, this to a security monitor in the refinery that was somehow still working. Foluke killed everyone she encountered.

Ayoola and Bolade were equally disgusted with what was happening—but Akanke and Sere were confused as to what the problem was.

Akanke was the one who expressed it. "That's standard mission procedure!"

"No it isn't!" Ayoola said. "We don't just kill whoever we feel like killing."

"Why not?" Sere asked. "We're Nide. We're *better* than everyone, that's what you kept telling us, Oranmiyan. And we're better than those flatbrains on Oshun!"

"That isn't what I've been telling you," Oranmiyan said.

Sere snorted. "That's what the *real* boss told us. You're just his cavalry chief, and you gotta do what *he* says, and so do we."

Abeje frowned. Now that Sere was saying that, she knew that there was in fact someone over Oranmiyan, and she got a clear image of him. She supposed she shouldn't have been surprised, but why had nobody mentioned that before?

"That's right!" Akanke yelled. "And I'm not gonna just sit here and get yelled at by some cavalry chief who don't know nothing about nothing!"

Akanke started to storm out of the lecture hall.

Then she stopped, and started screaming, Oranmiyan having seized her mind. "You ain't leavin' yet, Akanke."

Whirling around, Akanke grimaced and Oranmiyan suddenly stumbled back.

Sere put a hand on Akanke's shoulder and said, "Hey, Akanke, calm down, before you—"

Akanke grabbed Sere's jaw with her left hand and yanked it sharply to the right, snapping his neck with a crack that echoed throughout the lecture hall. He fell to the ground, dead, even as Ayoola ran over to her. Akanke gave her a kick to the stomach.

Getting to her feet, Abeje cried, "Akanke, what're you doing?"

"Don't even think about it, *buruku!*" Akanke yelled, and suddenly Abeje's brain was on fire. Screaming, she fell to her knees, gripping the sides of her head, wishing the pain away, screaming and screaming . . .

The report of a weapon deafened Abeje, but it also made the pain go away.

Stumbling to her feet, Abeje saw Ayoola doubled over and choking, Sere and Akanke both dead on the floor, the latter with a smoking hole in her chest.

In the center of the room stood Oranmiyan with his Ayoka still aimed at where Akanke had been standing.

Aside from Ayoola's coughing, nobody made a sound.

Eventually, Oranmiyan broke the silence. "Everyone out."

"Oranmiyan," Abeje started.

NOW! He projected that into everyone's mind so loud that Abeje instantly felt as if she had a migraine.

As she exited the lecture hall, she looked down at Akanke's body. She had always been so calm and reserved. Shango-oti turned her into this.

She was starting to wonder if Oranmiyan's sales pitch had left out a few important details.

Briefly, she turned to look back at him, but he was even more stone-faced than usual.

Maybe we'll be able to talk later.

As she left, she heard a voice sound over the speaker. "Vessel on approach. It's *L'owuro.*"

Abeje frowned. Wasn't that the cavalry ship Folami had been assigned to that was in orbit of Oshun?

TEN
L'owuro

YOU'RE STANDING IN THE MIDDLE of the Circle with Hembadoon. *The Orisha only summons trainees to this place in the middle of the forest outside the training facility to discuss matters of great import. Usually the Orisha dispenses wisdom, but today he is informing you that it is time for the final test. What some call the graduation exercise, Hembadoon called the final exam, and others called achieving the greatness they deserve. You are happier than you've ever been. Abeje is also thrilled, throwing a party in your honor that night with the other trainees. At last, the final exam!*

One mission to perform, after which you will become Ori-Inu.

(The Eso raises its claw.)

You've never met Oba Isembi before. Growing up on Yemoja, you had been fed endless propaganda about what a monster Isembi is, but the Oba is actually a very pleasant, older man with a thick beard, white hair tied back in a ponytail, and a strong bearing. He tells you that your mission is unique, one only you can perform because of your special knowledge of Olorun's inner sanctum in the heart of Nupe on Yemoja.

Your final mission to perform, after which you will become Ori-Inu.

(The Eso's claw starts to come down.)

*Your insertion onto Yemoja goes smoothly, with the help of
Hembadoon. The Orisha insists on providing support on his vessel,
Ebun, for which you are grateful. You've been training with
Hembadoon, and he knows how you fight, how you move. You work
your way through Olorun's edifice, the huge building where you spent
so much time, avoiding the very security systems you helped create.
At one point, you pass by the records room, and you find yourself
unable to resist looking up your own records, wondering what the
Oyo Empire's files had to say about you.*

*After which you will finish your final mission, and become Ori-
Inu.*

(The Eso claw comes straight for your head.)

*You find a file that includes a listing from your parents that makes
no sense. The name of your mother is the woman who raised you,
but the father is "Prisoner 92." A further check shows that Prisoner
92 was a man from the Olodumare Hegemony—one of the people on
whose ancestors the Hegemony did genetic experiments in the hopes
of breeding telepathy in their descendents. Olorun had captured him
and injected his seed into your mother, giving the Oyo Empire their
first-ever telepath.*

*You are suddenly much more motivated to finish your final
mission, after which you will become Ori-Inu.*

(The Eso claw bears down on you.)

*You confront Olorun. Now you know why your parents gave you
up so easily, why Olorun knew who you were, knew what you were
capable of. Abandoning all pretense of stealth, you mindblast everyone
in the sanctum—everyone except Olorun. You save him for last. You
want to look in his eyes when you kill him.*

After which, you will become Ori-Inu.

(You telekinetically thrust the Eso claw aside.)

But he laughs at you. He tells you that you're a stupid little girl and that you'll never harm him. Sure enough, you cannot mindblast him. "I am the ruler of the greatest empire in the history of humanity," he says. "Do you truly think I would create a weapon that I could not defend myself against?" He has a psi-screen greater than that of the Hegemony, even, and you cannot affect his mind.

You won't complete your mission, and you won't become Ori-Inu.

(You lock eyes with the Eso and mindblast him.)

Olorun continues to laugh. He laughs at your frustration, he laughs at your uselessness. "You are my weapon, little girl. No one else's. Through you, I will make the Hegemony fall and I will rule over all!" He laughs some more, and you cannot stand it.

You reach out with your telekinesis, shattering the alleged god's sanctum into billions of shards of metal and adobe.

The shrapnel rips through Olorun's all-too-human body, tearing it to pieces.

But you don't stop there.

Your mind reaches out further and further. You destroy Nupe, leveling the houses, offices, and especially the soccer stadium. You sink the continent on which it stands. You shatter Yemoja's crust, the mantle, the very heart of the world, snapping it in twain.

You have completed your mission, and you will die an Ori-Inu.

(But as it falls to the ground, it isn't one of the Oyo's genetically engineered killing machines.)

But you don't die. You've destroyed an entire world, physically changed the very face of the system forevermore, handed the greatest victory in the history of the Hegemony to Isembi—but somehow, after it's over, you wake up in a hospital on Ife. The finest doctors in the Hegemony have worked for more than a week to save you. Oba Isembi himself has commanded it, and he even visits you, calling you the greatest hero in Olodumare history.

Your mission is done, and you are Ori-Inu.

(It's Abeje. You've killed her.)

Eventually you learn that Hembadoon rescued you, steering Ebun through the collapsing planet, fighting fluctuating gravity, dodging rock and earth and fire, and somehow pulling you out of the wreckage that you created. The ship itself was nearly destroyed, and had been found by a Cavalry patrol that was investigating the destruction of Yemoja.

Once you have recovered, you are mindwiped as promised. Now you are truly Ori-Inu.

(She stares up at you with her dead eyes wondering why you, her closest friend, betrayed her.)

Your exploits as Ori-Inu soon become legendary. You accomplish every mission you're sent on without injury or difficulty. Your strength, your courage, your stamina, and your tenth-level mental abilities all combine to make you virtually unstoppable. Against any and all enemies of the Hegemony, you're unable to be defeated.

Especially against the Oyo. Isembi never passes up an opportunity to allow you to once again take your revenge on the Oyo by sending you to find the Eso and to assassinate their spies. Even though, since being mindwiped, you don't truly appreciate it.

(Another Eso comes up behind you.)

You walk the corridors of L'owuro. Recent events have you frightened, and you're not sure who to turn to. Cavalry Chief Adejola has been friendly to you, treating you like a person instead of an Ori-Inu. It's a novel experience, and since exposure to Shango-oti has made you start to remember life before being an Ori-Inu—life when you really were a person—maybe the one who's treated you like a person can help. So you approach Adejola's door, hoping to find release and comfort.

(He raises his claw.)

(You do nothing.)

(The claw comes right for your chest.)
(The claw is about to rip into your chest . . .)

Folami woke up screaming, the images fading from her mind.

The memories, though, remained this time. Much as she wished they didn't.

"Good, you're awake," came a dry voice from nearby.

Looking around, Folami saw that she was on a metal bunk. After a second, she realized that it was the brig of *L'owuro,* a room she'd only seen from the outside before. It was a featureless metal room, with the bunk and a commode on one wall, electrified bars on the opposite wall, and nothing on the other two walls, which were only two meters long.

Facing her was another cell, in which sat Orisha Hembadoon. It was he who'd spoken.

Looking down, Folami saw that she was still wearing the open bathrobe and underclothing she'd had on in Adejola's cabin. Hastily closing and tying the robe, she sat up and looked at Hembadoon. He was, surprisingly, still wearing his robes, though she noticed that there was some kind of device attached to his left temple.

"You saved me."

Hembadoon blinked. "I'm sorry?"

"It's taken a while for the Shango-oti to fully remove all the mindwipes. I still couldn't remember what my final exam was."

"And now you do?" Hembadoon winced and shook his head. "I'm sorry, Folami. Even if mindwiping hadn't been standard operating procedure, I would've insisted upon it for you after that. Nobody should have to remember doing what you did."

Folami found that she had nothing to say to that, so she tried to shove the memories into the back of her mind.

Conveniently, their current predicament made that easier than it might have been under other circumstances. Hembadoon himself had trained her to compartmentalize her thoughts in order to focus on the mission, and right now the mission had gone very much sideways.

"How'd we wind up here?"

"Your guess is as good as mine. I was in my cabin writing my report for Isembi when I fell asleep. I figure it was gas." He tapped the device on his temple. "Whoever it was knows what they're doing. They knew they couldn't get the robes off me, but this thing blocks my ability to interface with it. Right now, it's just an unflattering white drape."

Folami couldn't read Hembadoon's mind, of course, nor anything else. The cells in the brig were all equipped with psi-screens as a standard feature.

"Way I figure it," Hembadoon was saying, "someone boarded the ship, took over the flight deck, and used the intruder alert systems to gas us."

"But why us? We're the only ones in the brig."

Hembadoon shrugged. "Could be we're the only survivors. Unlike the cavalry, you and I are actually valuable hostages."

Folami didn't even dignify that with a response. Orisha and Ori-Inu were expendable, as any idiot who tried to kidnap one realized in fairly short order.

"Of course, they may not want us as hostages, but to question us."

That deserved even less of a response. Folami doubted the interrogation technique existed that could pry information out of a tenth-level.

"There's another possibility," she said quietly. "The Nide."

"What, the hyped-up Ori-Inu?" Hembadoon asked.

Folami nodded. "Oranmiyan tried to recruit me on Oshun. And they're all Ori-Inu who were taken. Maybe they want me."

"Doesn't explain why they kept *me* alive. Or why they'd use the intruder systems. Folks like that can just barrel their way in. Taking over the flight deck, gassing people—that's a military strategy, not an Ori-Inu strategy."

As Hembadoon said that last sentence, the door to the brig opened to reveal Adejola and War Chief Tobi. The fact that they were unharmed and walking freely about the ship meant that there was a fourth possibility, one that Folami didn't like in the least.

"Good job there, Orisha," Tobi said with a grin. "I'm starting to understand why Isembi thinks so highly of you."

Adejola looked at Folami. "I'm sorry, Folami, truly."

"If you'd just stayed in your damned quarters," Tobi said to Folami, "everything would've been fine." Then he turned his glare onto Adejola. "Instead, you had to choose tonight to get some company."

Hembadoon sat up straighter at that for some reason.

Folami, however, was more concerned with what this was all about. She had considered and rejected the notion of Tobi betraying her and Hembadoon because she had never, in all the time she'd been on *L'owuro*, sensed any kind of ill intentions along these lines from Tobi. A treason of this magnitude couldn't simply be hid, not by a flatbrain.

Tobi threw his head back and laughed. "Oh, I have to tell you, Ori-Inu, seeing that look of confusion on your face is the most wonderful sight I've seen all year. You'll be happy to know that the farce of 'searching' for Olokun Station has been abandoned. We're heading straight there now."

Hembadoon nodded. "You know where Olokun Station is."

Based on his tone, Hembadoon had put it together—so had Folami. "You *run* Olokun Station," she said. "Ojiji—you're the one in charge?"

The war chief clapped sardonically at that. "Very good, both of you. And the reason why your precious Oba didn't know about it is because we're hardly going to tell the *buruku* we want to overthrow about the project designed to overthrow him."

Now Hembadoon rolled his eyes. "You have *got* to be kidding me. *That's* what this is all about?"

Tobi looked witheringly at Hembadoon. "That's what *everything's* about, Hembadoon—power. Isembi doesn't deserve it. No flatbrain does."

Folami started. "No."

Looking back at Folami, Tobi grinned. "Ah, now the Ori-Inu finally starts to understand."

Hembadoon was shaking his head. "Here I thought I always got a bigger headache around you 'cause of your loud-ass voice."

Frowning, Folami said, "I've read your file, you're a second-level."

"It's easy to fake records if you're good enough, especially back then when the procedures for finding telepaths weren't as efficient as they are now. And," he added with a vicious smile, "I've *always* been more than good enough."

Hembadoon looked at Adejola. "So you were just coming on to Folami to help soften her up?"

"No!" Adejola said defensively. "Honestly, I just wanted to—"

"Shut *up*, Cavalry Chief," Tobi said. "Believe me, Hembadoon, if it was up to me, this fool wouldn't have gotten within a meter of the Ori-Inu. She's just a tool, nothing more."

"Really?" Folami asked. "Funny, Oranmiyan was going on about how Nide are free."

"Nide aren't Ori-Inu," Tobi said tightly.

Folami noticed that that didn't actually address her point. *Is Oranmiyan just another tool, too?*

However, before she could pursue the matter, Modupe's voice sounded over the intercom. "Infirmary to War Chief Tobi."

Looking up, the war chief said, "Tobi."

"We're ready to do the Ori-Inu's surgery, sir."

"Good. Send the medtechs down for her."

Folami stared incredulously at Tobi. "The doctor's in on this?"

"He is now. You'd be amazed how much you can accomplish with threats to a weak-willed person, Ori-Inu."

Hembadoon shook his head. "Threats only work if you're going to follow through on them, War Chief—and even if you do that, you have to be ready to pay the consequences."

"Oh, don't worry, Orisha—I'm more than willing to actually kill Modupe's wife and daughter, *and* if I do there are guaranteed to be no consequences whatsoever."

But Folami didn't care about that. She was using Hembadoon's outrage as a cover to concentrate.

Hembadoon, bless him, kept talking, engaging the war chief's attention for a few precious seconds. "I'm curious as to why *I'm* still breathing, War Chief. Folami's your latest recruit, I understand that, but what does keeping me alive get you? Not that I'm complaining, mind you."

In essence what Folami was doing was isolating her mind from the rest of her body. It wasn't something she could do for very long without risking permanent brain damage or death, but if they were about to take her for surgery of some kind, she needed to be prepared.

"Oh, you have your uses, Hembadoon," Tobi was saying. "I know your loyalty to Isembi is fleeting at best. And you have other skills I can use."

"You don't know the first thing about me or my loyalty, War Chief. And I owe a lot more to Isembi than I do to your murdering ass."

"We'll see," Tobi said with a smile. Then he turned to Adejola. "Do it."

The pilot activated a control, and seconds later, Folami started to get the same dizzy feeling she had in his cabin.

They were gassing her.

But this time she'd be ready.

The gas still had an immediate reaction, putting her body to sleep, but she had managed to telepathically keep most of her brain safe from the gas, leaving her clear-headed.

She faded in and out of awareness.

One moment, she felt the arms of two of Modupe's medtechs picking her up and removing her bathrobe and underclothes, replacing them with a hospital gown.

The next, she was floating in a featureless void.

Then she was sitting in the dining hall during training—but she was dining with three Eso.

Then she was back in the void, but with Oranmiyan and Hembadoon alongside her, and the three of them were playing a card game.

Then she was being brought down a *L'owuro* corridor on a gurney, the medtechs checking her vitals.

Then she attended her tenth birthday, the last birthday she had at her home in Nupe before her parents gave her over to Olorun. Tobi and Abeje were at that party, and they really enjoyed the soup.

Then she was in the corridor that led to the infirmary.

Then she was back in the void—

—but she *couldn't be in the void!* She had to come back! *Come back!*

Hembadoon, Oranmiyan, the Eso, Olorun, her parents, they all yelled at her to come back!

Then she sat up on the gurney, slamming her hand into the throat of one of the medtechs while kicking the other one in the gut, both moves that would render them incapable of speech for at least a few minutes.

Not that it mattered, as it turned out that Tobi remained cautious and intelligent. Four cavalry had been assigned to guard her as she was transported to the infirmary. Three of them were cavalrypeople she had saved from the Eso down on Oshun: Kehinde, Juhoke, and Iwohu. The fourth was their CO, Cavalry Chief Olugbanma.

However, they hadn't been expecting the patient to leap up out of nowhere and attack the medtechs, either. So they wasted a precious second being shocked before they raised their weapons.

Juhoke and Iwohu were in front of the gurney, with Olugbanma and Kehinde behind. Kehinde and Olugbanma only needed to fire, where Iwohu and Juhoke also needed to turn around, so she went after the cavalry chief and Kehinde first.

Consciously not wrinkling her nose (*and thank you, Oranmiyan, for letting me know about that tell . . .*), Folami concentrated and telekinetically tore the pair's Ayokas into a dozen pieces.

As for Iwohu and Juhoke, she sent them both careening down the corridor, after yanking their Ayokas from their hands.

Kehinde was on the deck, cradling his hands, which had been injured by the exploding weapon even through his armor, but Olugbanma had whipped out his sidearm, a Bayo pistol.

Before she could fire, Folami telekinetically fired the two Ayokas she'd grabbed from Juhoke and Iwohu, shooting half a dozen rounds from each one at Olugbanma, who was knocked back to the deck, the chestplate of his armor ripped to shreds.

She hadn't wanted to kill anyone, and so far she hadn't. These men and women had fought alongside her against the Eso just a few days ago, and she wouldn't kill them now without reason. She did, however, short out and shut down the armor of all three cavalrypeople, rendering them useless.

Hesitating, she scanned all six of them. The medtechs and the cavalrypeople were simply following orders, and were unaware of the existence of Ojiji beyond possibly seeing it in a recent report or overhearing it on board.

Cavalry Chief Olugbanma, however, was on the program. And Folami's scan revealed that most of the higher-ranks on board were fully aware of what War Chief Tobi was doing. The lower ranks weren't, but they also generally weren't dumb enough to openly question their superiors.

Olugbanma was groaning on the deck, and Folami knelt down next to him. "You tell Tobi, Cavalry Chief, that Ojiji's finished. I'm going to destroy it."

"*Buruku* . . ." The cavalry chief then coughed up blood.

Getting to her feet, Folami reloaded the two Ayokas, grabbed some more spare ammo, then mentally ripped the remaining weapons to tiny pieces.

A headache started to slice into her skull behind her right eye. *Gotta take it easy*, she thought. *You're armed now—use the guns, save the psionic tricks for when you need them.*

With the upper ranks on Tobi's side, staying on *L'owuro* was suicide. She needed backup and she needed to get off the ship in order to call for it.

No alert had gone off, but eventually someone would notice that she hadn't made it to the infirmary. If nothing else, Modupe would probably whine to Tobi asking where his patient was.

Instinctively, she tried to interface with the ship's computer, but of course, she wasn't wearing her body armor. She considered and rejected returning to her quarters to retrieve it. Her cabin was on another deck, and it would take too long to get there, and then to the dropship bay.

No, a dropship won't do any good. Range is too limited. Same with the escape pods.

The flight deck was just a few meters from here, though. If she disabled the control systems there—which would require *massive* use of her telekinesis—then she'd be able to move more freely about the ship *and* escape without *L'owuro* being able to track her.

Which still left the question of *what* she could escape in.

As she made her way toward the flight deck, she remembered Hembadoon. Unfortunately, rescuing him was an even worse idea than retrieving her battle suit. Taking out four surprised cavalry and one medtech was one thing, but an entire ship of cavalry was more than she could handle alone.

I'm sorry, Hembadoon.

Then it hit her: Hembadoon had come here in his ship! It was the very same ship he'd brought her to Yemoja in, and the very same ship—

Tears welled up in her eyes, the new memories bleeding forth from the back of her mind. He had *Ebun*, the ship he'd brought her to Yemoja on, and the ship he'd rescued her with. She had been in recovery for months after that, and it had taken longer for the techs to fix *Ebun*. Isembi would have given him a new ship, but he insisted on keeping that one.

Best of all, an Orisha's ship would respond to the commands of an Ori-Inu. And because it wasn't assigned to *L'owuro*, it didn't carry the risks of taking one of Tobi's own vessels that he might have modified for his own use.

As she approached the door to the flight deck, it slid open. Even with *L'owuro* at GQ, the flight deck door wasn't secured—that would only happen in case of a security alert, which would be sounding any second now.

The personnel on duty all turned to look at the beautiful woman wearing only a hospital gown and holding up two Ayokas.

She fired one shot from each of the rifles into the ceiling to get everyone's attention—not that she didn't have it already.

Cavalry Master Ama was in command of the deck, and rose to her feet from the tactical station. "What're you doing, you crazy *buruku*?"

"I suggest you all move away from your consoles."

Then she shut down each station on the flight deck.

Surge protectors kept the consoles from sparking and burning, but only barely. Displays went down, controls stopped responding, static filled the speakers, and holographs went dark.

The one surge protector that failed was the tac console, which literally blew up in Ama's face.

For one second, the deck was silent.

Then: "Scanners down!" "Helm not responding!" "I can't get a fix!" "Nothing's working!" "*Mogbe*!"

Folami turned around, waited for the door to shut, then mentally adjusted the controls so that the flight deck was in lockdown mode.

She wiped her nose with the gown sleeve, and blood came off onto it. The spike behind her eye was now a drill. *Okay, that's definitely the last psi trick for a while.*

Running barefoot through the corridors proved mildly painful, as her feet were unaccustomed to functioning without the boots that maximized comfort and minimized stress injuries in the field. The unyielding metal slamming into the balls of her feet as she ran was going to be a problem if she kept it up.

A klaxon sounded, indicating that somebody had either noticed that she was missing, that the flight deck was cut off from the rest of the ship, or both. Either way, she just had to get to the dropship bay and she was clear.

About thirty meters from the bay doors, she sensed two cavalrymen on guard. They stood at attention but were bored to death. They'd gotten this assignment because they were caught playing cards while on duty.

Sorry about this, but telekinesis is not an option right now.

As soon as they were in sight, she shot them each with her borrowed Ayokas.

Like Olugbanma, they would live if they got medical attention soon, though their armor was shot to pieces.

The bay door didn't open at her approach, and she didn't have her body armor to interface, so she had to manually enter her Ori-Inu ID and allow the computer to scan her biometrics.

Once that was done, the door obediently slid aside for her.

Sure enough, there was a one-person craft, standard issue for Orisha in the field.

She approached, activated the hatch and climbed in. The

startup sequence was simple enough, and her Ori-Inu priority started the procedure to depressurize the bay and open the bay doors. The only way it could have been overridden was from the flight deck, and that wasn't happening any time soon.

As the air was blown out of the bay, equalizing the pressure with that of the vacuum of space, Tobi's voice came over the intercom. "Security alert! The Ori-Inu has gone renegade and the flight deck has been compromised! She is considered a first-class target."

Folami smiled grimly. A first-class target was to be killed on sight. *I guess I should be flattered.*

However, Folami had, naturally, done her job well. Tobi had no idea she was on Hembadoon's ship, nor that she was making her escape via the dropship bay.

By the time the flight deck was operational again, she would be long gone from *L'owuro*'s sensors.

And then she would start working on a plan to keep her promise to Cavalry Chief Olugbanma to stop Ojiji.

ELEVEN
Olokun Station

As soon as War Chief Tobi—the head of Ojiji—set foot onto Olokun Station after *L'owuro* docked, Abeje knew something was wrong.

Folami wasn't here.

Based on the look on Oranmiyan's face next to her, he had come to the same realization.

Olokun Station was buried inside an asteroid—one of the remnants of the destruction of Yemoja. Since returning from Oshun, Abeje had taken a tour of the facility and been very impressed. War Chief Tobi had had an engine installed inside the rock of the asteroid, and the facility built elsewhere, with sophisticated scan blockers combining with the mineral composition of the asteroid to confuse scans. Not that anyone usually wasted their time scanning one asteroid that looked like every other piece of Yemoja that was floating around.

After the docking procedure was complete, War Chief Tobi had stepped through the airlock. Abeje knew who Tobi was, but she had never been assigned to Rufiji, so she'd never met him. He was much taller than she'd imagined, and his personnel image didn't convey the fury in his hazel eyes.

Though she figured the latter had to do with Folami's disappearance.

"What happened?" Oranmiyan asked without preamble.

"We need to use Olokun's scanners to try to find the Orisha's ship."

"I asked you a question, War Chief," Oranmiyan said tightly.

Tobi stared at Oranmiyan. "And I gave you an order. Kindly follow it. The Ori-Inu escaped in the Orisha's ship and sabotaged L'owuro on her way out the door. We have to find her."

Oranmiyan started. He had told Abeje that radio silence was standard operating procedure for Tobi when he was approaching Olokun, but now it seemed that that silence was enforced this time.

Folding his large arms over his larger chest, Oranmiyan said, "You told me that I shouldn't take on Folami down on Oshun. You told me it was too risky, that she was too good. You told me you'd have it easier, since she'd be at ease on L'owuro instead of fighting every step of the way against me and my Nide. So I'm asking you again, War Chief, what *happened?*"

Tobi stared stonily at Oranmiyan. "In case you've forgotten, I don't report to you. This is *my* project, and I don't appreciate your tone. Modify it."

"I could've taken Folami myself. I had her half a dozen times on Oshun, but I let her go because *you* said so. You *did* sedate her, right?"

"Of course we did," Tobi said tightly, "but she beat it somehow."

"You use anatherizine, like I told you?"

"There was no need to waste it. That stuff's expensive, and we've got plenty of hathronol as part of our standard security system."

Oranmiyan threw his head back and laughed. It was a scary

laugh, one that made Abeje nervous. But she also understood why he was reacting that way, though she was starting to think that the anger was better.

The laugh reminded her far too much of Akanke.

"Something amuses you?" Tobi asked frostily.

Abeje decided to speak up before the tension between the two men came to blows. "One of the first tricks Hembadoon taught us was how to beat hathronol. Not all telepaths can do it, but Folami nailed it pretty early on."

"Which is why I told you *not* to use it!" Oranmiyan was yelling now. "Let me guess, she waited until she was in a corridor, took out the medics and any guards you had on her before they could call for backup, then went to the flight deck and wiped all the systems, then she was gone before you even knew anything happened, right? And I bet she didn't kill anyone, either, because she's sweet like that."

Putting his hands on his hips, Tobi asked, "How did you know *that*?"

"I *trained* with her! I know how her mind works, which is why *I* should've been the one taking her in!"

"We'll find her. Meanwhile, I've got something for you to do. Your precious Orisha Hembadoon is in the brig. He's a sensitive, and he was exposed to Shango-oti. I want to know what the full effects were on him. He doesn't seem to have any of the instability we've come across."

"We've done more than 'come across' it, War Chief. I had to put down Akanke after she went crazy. She killed Sere and hurt Ayoola before I could stop her."

"It happens," Tobi said with a shrug. "How many you get on Oshun?"

"None."

His face contorting into a rictus of fury, Tobi cried, "What!? I thought the 'deaths' that the Ori-Inu reported were ones your people covered up!"

"No, they just were going on a killing spree—Ori-Inu *and* civilians!"

The two started moving toward each other. Abeje was nervous, in part because she could feel the tension between them, but mostly because she *couldn't* feel anything of their minds. Tobi was as closed to her as Oranmiyan was.

"You've been messing with me from the start, haven't you, War Chief?" Oranmiyan's eyes had gone wild, and spittle was flying out of his mouth as he yelled. "Shango-oti can't do most of what you told me it does, can it?"

"I've never lied to you," Tobi said. "Shango-oti does *exactly* what I said it would: enhance a person's telepathy and make them better and stronger." He looked at Abeje. "Isn't that right?"

"Uhm . . ." Abeje really didn't want to get between those two, and now may not have been the best time to voice her second thoughts. However, that glower from the war chief was hard to resist. "Well, yes, it has done that. But I also saw what it did to Akanke."

Tobi shrugged. "Some people can't handle it. People are at a certain level for a reason—maybe for some people, having it go too high makes them insane. Whatever, it doesn't matter—are we gonna just stand here yelling at each other, or are we going to actually *accomplish* something?"

Hembadoon was brought in shackles through the corridors of *L'owuro* to the docking bay, and thence through several corridors hewn out of natural rock toward a sterile-looking room that had a small operating table, onto which he was placed and put into restraints.

The two cavalry who had escorted him left, and then two other people entered whom he knew very well—but only one of whom was supposed to still be alive.

"Oranmiyan—I don't know whether to hug you or punch you. These shackles solve my dilemma, of course. Still, I could have *sworn* I led a memorial service for you."

"I'm glad you did, Orisha." Oranmiyan was sneering at him. This was *not* the polite, eager young man he'd found in the slums of Benin and trained until his—alleged—death. "It meant my deception worked."

"You'll have to tell me about that some time." He turned to Abeje. "As for you, I have to confess to being quite impressed with myself."

Abeje stared at him incredulously. "How so?"

"After everything I've been through the last week, I have at last completed my mission. How many Orisha do you know who can bring it home after living through an explosion, being gassed twice, and then being led in irons to a secret mobile facility disguised as an asteroid?"

Oranmiyan frowned. "Tobi told you all of that?"

"Actually, I worked it out on my own. That's why the Hegemony pays me so well, though Tobi did confirm it after he gassed me and Folami."

"That *idiot!*" Oranmiyan slammed a fist into the metal wall. To Hembadoon's surprise—and fear—it left a small dent in the wall, which was strong enough to keep an entire asteroid from caving in on the room.

He was never this strong before. Nor this temperamental. What happened to him?

"Oranmiyan, calm down," Abeje said, putting a hand on his shoulder.

Hembadoon watched the dynamic of his former pupils, who had been lovers in a previous life. Abeje obviously still had deep feelings for Oranmiyan. But the Orisha wasn't sure if those feelings were returned.

"The whole thing's completely messed up," Oranmiyan said. "Shango-oti is supposed to make us *free*!"

"Free, eh?" Hembadoon said. "Free to do what, precisely? Commit mass murder? Or were all those bodies on Oshun merely the cost of doing business?"

"Shut up!" Oranmiyan stomped over to Hembadoon and shoved a finger in his face. "You don't know what you're talking about."

But Hembadoon saw Abeje shrinking away from Oranmiyan, and saw her react to what the Orisha had said. "That wasn't part of the plan, was it, Oranmiyan? It was just to be a smash and grab. But they smashed too much, yes? I'm guessing that Shango-oti does more than hype up your mental capacity. I'm thinking it also makes you a little crazy."

"I said *shut up*!" Oranmiyan backhanded Hembadoon. He winced with the impact, and felt a burning on his left cheek.

"You weren't like this before, Oranmiyan. You were always the calm voice of reason. Now you're ready to explode. If it's not the Shango-oti, what is it?"

"Oranmiyan," Abeje said gently, "maybe he's right. I remember what Akanke was like before."

"Of course I'm right," Hembadoon said insistently. "When was I ever wrong?"

"You don't understand," Oranmiyan said, looking as if he was trying to get his breathing under control. "Shango-oti is the *key*. We can stop being puppets of the Oba! We can be free!"

"You keep saying that," Abeje said, "but how are we free, exactly? We're hiding in an asteroid, half of us are going crazy, and for what? So that *buruku* can take over from Isembi and start it all over again?"

"Shut *up*!" Oranmiyan cried. "That is *not* the plan!" His attempts to get his breathing under control were failing.

"That's not what he told Folami and me," Hembadoon said. "Told us he wanted to take over from Isembi, and that he'd be using the Nide to do it. Just another set of tools, he said. Looks to me like you're trading in one oppressor for another."

Abeje walked up to him and put her small arm in his big one. "He's right, Oranmiyan. This isn't what you told me it was going to be."

We're getting through to him, Hembadoon thought, grateful that he had Abeje on his side, at least.

Then Oranmiyan threw his head back, roared, and cried, "NO!"

He flexed his arms, and Abeje went flying toward the wall, hitting it with a sickening crunch.

"You don't understand!" Oranmiyan yelled at her crumpled form. "We *will* be free! We'll get Folami back and then we'll all be back together and it'll be like it was *supposed* to be! We'll save the universe from the bad guys, just like we were saying we'd be doing! Don't you get it, Abeje? Don't you?"

Hembadoon's hopes had all been dashed with one gesture, because Abeje wasn't responding to Oranmiyan's imploring.

Having been an Orisha for most of his adult life, Hembadoon had seen plenty of dead bodies. He quickly learned to tell the difference between the living and the dead, and the primary one was that dead bodies were completely still. The living shuddered or shivered or twitched or blinked or moved in *some* way. But the dead didn't move at all.

And right now, Abeje wasn't moving at all.

"She's dead."

Oranmiyan's face fell. "No. She can't . . ." He bent down and turned her body over, only to reveal her head at an impossible angle in relation to her neck.

Tears were now streaming down Oranmiyan's cheeks. "No . . . Abeje, you can't die. That wasn't the plan . . ."

That went on for several seconds—Oranmiyan kneeling over Abeje's body and muttering to himself, tears flowing freely. Hembadoon lay on the surgical table, tugging uselessly against his unbreakable restraints, and wondering what what was going to happen next.

He didn't have to wonder for long. Oranmiyan sprang to his feet, and started screaming incoherently, storming out of the room.

Hembadoon lay on the surgical table, alone with the corpse of one of his prize pupils, whose only crime was to tell another of his prize pupils that things were going badly. And he had no idea where his third prize pupil was now.

This isn't exactly going the way I'd hoped, he thought angrily. Instead of having two Nide on his side, he now had one dead and another descending further into madness.

And he was still strapped to a surgical table.

I hope you're coming back soon, Folami, Hembadoon thought.

TWELVE
Ebun

FOLAMI WAITED UNTIL SHE WAS sure that *Ebun* was out of what would be *L'owuro's* scanning range were her scanners working before she brought the engines to a halt, left the ship drifting, and then broke down crying.

Up until now, her training had kept her going, allowed her to get information, allowed her to make her escape.

But now that that was done, she needed a release.

She'd been hoping to get that from Cavalry Chief Adejola, but his was merely the latest in a long line of betrayals that started with her mother allowing Olorun to use her as an incubator for a telepath, went on to Oranmiyan making everyone think he was dead, and ending with Adejola gassing her.

Could be worse, I suppose, she thought, *he could've had sex with me and then gassed me.*

After a moment, that thought made her burst out laughing, even as the tears continued to stream down her face. Her halting sobs mixed with laughs and led to a coughing fit.

A full minute passed before she was able to wipe her eyes dry with the sleeve of her hospital gown and get her breathing under control.

She also realized that she was hungry.

Bereft of armor to interface with *Ebun*'s computer, she instead used her Ori-Inu priority to re-set it to accept voice commands.

"Computer, provisions."

A screen lit up with a list of available foodstuffs and a location: an orange, a bunch of grapes, and a pair of cocoa cookies, all in a refrigerator located under the console; a bottle of wine in a cabinet in the ceiling; and water from a spigot next to her.

"Computer, commode?"

A control on the console lit up. Touching it released a catheter.

"Wonderful."

She allowed herself five minutes to get some food in her system and relieve herself. Ideally, she would have liked a few hours' sleep, but that wasn't going to be possible. Still, she was mindful of one of this ship's owner's many aphorisms: "The human body's like a ship. You don't put fuel in it, it ain't goin' anywhere."

After cleaning out Hembadoon's entire supply of fruit and cookies, washing it down with some refreshingly cold water (some of which she also splashed on her face), she finally went ahead and contacted Ife.

It took ten minutes for her to work her way through various functionaries and for said functionaries to find the Oba before Isembi's face appeared before her.

Part of why Folami had delayed the call until after she ate something was to settle her stomach, because the idea of facing this man made her want to throw up. For all that he called her a hero after she destroyed Yemoja, the mindwipe meant that he could take all the credit for it.

Not that she particularly *wanted* to claim responsibility,

but the glee with which Oba Isembi had added "destroyer of Yemoja" to his many titles sickened her, all the more because he didn't actually do it.

She was also grateful that she had not told Isembi about her remembering things, because at least one of those unburied memories involved actions taken by the Oba that he would definitely not want made public. Out of self-preservation as much as anything, she needed to keep that from him.

However, she was still a loyal Ori-Inu, and she also needed backup in order to bring Ojiji down.

As soon as he saw Folami, Isembi's face fell. "Folami, what happened?"

"Quite a bit," she said.

Concisely, but leaving out no details save that of her own reawakening memories (and of her visiting Cavalry Chief Adejola's quarters, since that wasn't germane to the report, not to mention being horribly embarrassing), she informed Isembi of the events since their last report.

"Tobi a traitor? Amazing." Isembi shook his head. "I would never have thought—" He let out a quick breath. "But of course he would not have gotten this far if I suspected him. And from the sounds of it, this particular plan is many years in the making."

"My Oba—" She said that phrase out of rote habit, but calling Isembi "her" Oba made her nauseous. "—I only left *L'owuro* to regroup and to summon reinforcements, something I couldn't do as long as I was in Tobi's scan range. As soon as you can send me a cadre of Ori-Inu, we can take Olokun Station and bring Ojiji down."

"I'm afraid it's more complicated than that. I sent all the available proximate Ori-Inu to Oshun already. Of the remaining

Ori-Inu, they're all either in the midst of missions that they can't be removed from, or are sufficiently far away that they won't arrive for another week or more."

"*Mogbe*," Folami muttered, before remembering who she was talking to. "Apologies, my Oba, but it's been very trying."

"I understand," Isembi said with uncharacteristic gentleness.

Folami didn't believe his sincerity for a second, but that was only because of what she now remembered.

"My Oba—we can't wait a week. We can't even wait another day. Tobi knows that he's been exposed. He'll go to ground, and he can take this station anywhere in the system. If he brings it to the main asteroid field where—where Yemoja used to be before—before you destroyed it, we'll never find it." She hoped that Isembi assumed her hesitation to be due to stress at the situation.

Isembi hesitated. "Folami, I can't ask you to do that. It'll be suicide. You against who knows how many of these Nide—and without your body armor!"

"The suit's just a tool, my Oba. And there's no choice. The safety of the Hegemony is at stake."

In truth, Folami didn't give a damn about the safety of the Hegemony right now. What she wanted was revenge on Tobi and Oranmiyan and everyone else who made her remember what she'd worked so hard to forget.

She'd get that revenge, or die trying. Either way was fine with her at this point.

Isembi regarded her for several seconds.

Finally, he said, "Part of me is tempted to order you to return to Ife. The risks are too great for you to even attempt such a mission by yourself, especially without your armor—and for all that it's a tool, it's a vital one." Isembi leaned back, stroking his beard. "However, the risks are even greater if Ojiji is allowed to continue to operate. I hereby approve your mission, Folami. Good luck."

Folami was grateful that he'd given the order to go on the mission, as it saved her the trouble of disobeying an order not to. "Thank you, my Oba."

As soon as Isembi's face faded, the yawn that Folami had been stifling practically split her face in half. "Computer," she said when she was done, "medical supplies."

The screen lit up with a list of *Ebun's* impressive pharmacopeia. She pocketed two stimulants.

Setting a course back to Olokun at *Ebun's* minimum speed, she started cogitating on possible strategies. Her scan of Olugbanma had revealed that there were about a half-dozen Nide on Olokun, plus Tobi and his crew, plus additional support staff. And the station itself was embedded in a big rock, which made a direct approach difficult.

So she'd have to take an indirect approach. An Ori-Inu's best skill was the ability to move without being noticed. Without her armor, she couldn't engage in a formal stealth mode, but that didn't preclude her ability to move undetected.

"Computer, emergency supplies list."

As expected, *Ebun* had an EVA suit, with a two-hour air supply. Checking the size, she breathed a sigh of relief that she was unusually tall for her sex—and that Hembadoon was only of average height. The suit would fit her.

"Computer, portable armament."

That list was shorter than she'd been hoping, but Orisha didn't generally need much more than a sidearm. Luckily, he kept a spare Bayo pistol and lots of spare ammunition on board, plus Folami had the two Ayokas she'd liberated from Iwohu and Juhoke. There were also two grenades, which might prove handy.

After checking their ETA to Olokun's expected position, she said, "Computer, wake me in forty-seven minutes." *Ebun* would be in scanning range of Olokun in fifty-seven minutes, and Folami figured she wouldn't need more than ten minutes to get her plan ready.

Laying back in the pilot seat, she closed her eyes and hoped she could doze without nightmares.

THIRTEEN
L'owuro

TOBI SAT IN HIS CABIN and sipped from a wide round glass filled with brandy. Tobi's choices in drinks always varied depending on his mood. If he was happy, he went for mead. If he was pensive, then he drank wine. If he was celebrating, he drank beer, simply because he liked to celebrate for a long time and beer had less of a deleterious effect on him. Tobi liked drinking, but didn't like to get drunk. Too much alcohol, and you lost control.

Tobi's survival depended on complete control.

When he was in a bad mood, that was when he opened the bottle of brandy. And his mood was particularly foul right now.

He stared at the wall filled with weapons he'd collected over the decades. It was an affectation, the gun collecting, one he'd begun not due to any great desire to collect hand weapons, but a desire to provide himself with a quirk, something to distract people from his true self.

In truth, the ritualized drinking was part of that as well. If people knew that he chose his alcohol based on mood, if they knew that he obsessively tracked down hand weapons, then they labored under the delusion that they knew who he was.

Of course, they had no idea.

He'd spent so many years building up War Chief Tobi that there were times that he almost forgot his true self.

That was why he kept Olokun Station mobile. This way it was always within reach, and he could remind himself who he really was.

He touched the intercom, which soon prompted the response: "Flight deck."

"Status report, Cavalryman."

"Consoles for navigation, tactical, and all scanning systems are fully repaired. Secondary consoles still under repair."

"Any sign of the Orisha ship?"

"Not as yet, sir."

Tobi snarled.

"Sir?"

"Nothing, Cavalryman. Out."

He stabbed the intercom control dolefully.

Damned Ori-Inu. Everything had been going so well until Folami was assigned to *L'owuro.*

At first, Tobi had been thrilled. Folami was a prime candidate for becoming a Nide, both because of her obscenely high telepathy level and because she was Isembi's pride and joy, his finest agent. By recruiting her to Ojiji, he would at once improve his own position and weaken his enemy's. Oranmiyan had also spoken highly of her, based on their time training together, and thought that he would be able to work with her to bring her over to their side.

But she had proven difficult. For starters, she actually *enjoyed* being an Ori-Inu. Most agents accepted their lot in life, but few showed Folami's enthusiasm.

Plus Tobi couldn't actually *read* her.

Bad enough he couldn't read Oranmiyan—but nobody

could, ever since that incident when he was a trainee. Oranmiyan couldn't be read, couldn't be mindwiped. It made him a useful ally and a powerful foe.

Not being able to read Folami, though, made it difficult to find the right way to bring her over. Worse, she was too talented to simply be subdued—as she had proven when she escaped from *L'owuro*.

"Flight deck to War Chief Tobi."

With a sigh, Tobi finished off his brandy, placed the glass down with a light clunk, and reactivated the intercom. "Tobi."

"Sir, Doctor Ogumefu on Olokun is requesting to speak with you. He says it's urgent."

Had it been Modupe with an urgent call, Tobi wouldn't have bothered, as *L'owuro*'s medical officer had a very different definition of *urgent* than Tobi did. However, Ogumefu was not one for hyperbole. In fact, he mostly preferred to stay out of Tobi's way and simply do what he was told, which was why Tobi had recruited him for Ojiji in the first place.

"Put him through."

"Yes, sir."

"War Chief, this is Doctor Ogumefu," came a voice in clipped tones. "I just arrived at the medical quarters, and there's a bit of a problem. Orisha Hembadoon is still present, but there's the corpse of a Nide on the ground—I believe it's the new recruit, Abeje. According to the security feed, Oranmiyan went mad and killed her."

Tobi put his head in his hands. "Thank you, Doctor. Have a detail of cavalry dispose of the body and you proceed with the Orisha."

"Very well."

"Good. Also, I think it's time we boxed up. Olokun's no

longer tenable. Let's have Apara pack away the Nide and prepare for a move to the second site."

"Very well, but that limits how much of an examination I can do of Orisha Hembadoon."

"Get started at least. It'll be a few hours before we'll be ready. Keep me apprised of your progress. Out."

Tobi then alerted the flight deck to put out a security alert for Oranmiyan and have him report to him on *L'owuro*.

He sighed. The war chief had known the risks with Shango-oti, but he had been informed by scientists who claimed to know what they were talking about that it would only adversely affect one in five telepaths.

However, it seemed that that those scientists were talking out of their hindquarters. Oranmiyan succumbing to the madness was particularly disturbing, as he was one of the first exposed, and his stability had been a major contributing factor to Tobi's decision to go ahead and make the Shango-oti widespread among the Ori-Inu he'd recruited.

Not that Oranmiyan had been much of an asset of late in any event. Tobi had had to go around Oranmiyan to make sure that the Nide on Oshun eliminated anyone who had been exposed to Shango-oti in the refinery explosion.

Damned Oyo spies, ruining my plans. And now I have to lose the station. He had a backup in place, of course, but the second site wasn't mobile the way Olokun was. It meant that Ojiji's options would be more limited.

With luck, though, Ogumefu would be able to figure out what it was about Hembadoon that was different. Unlike the other people who'd been exposed to Shango-oti, Hembadoon's telepathy only went up a single level, despite full exposure to the gas.

Of course, it could just have been an anomaly about the Orisha. But it was worth having Ogumefu run a few tests before they killed him.

Or maybe recruited him. For all his bluster, Tobi knew that Hembadoon would be willing to betray Isembi if the circumstances were appropriate. There was no better finder or trainer of telepaths alive, and when Tobi ruled, he would need someone with those talents.

"Flight deck to War Chief Tobi."

"Now, what?" he muttered, getting up to pour some more brandy. "Tobi."

"Sir, we've found *Ebun*!"

Tobi dropped the bottle of brandy, ignoring the expensive liquid that splashed all over the floor as the thick glass shattered against the metal deck. "I'm on my way. Disengage from Olokun immediately and pursue."

The war chief set a land-speed record getting to the flight deck. As soon as he entered, Cavalry Master Ama said, "War Chief on deck!"

"Status report," Tobi barked as he took his seat.

Ama said, "We've detected *Ebun* on an intercept course with Olokun. ETA in twenty minutes."

"Not hardly." Tobi looked at the main viewer, which was at its default of a forward view, which showed that *L'owuro* was still attached to Olokun. "Cavalry Chief Adejola, why aren't we moving?"

Adejola didn't miss a beat. "Docking clamps disengaging in five, War Chief. Three, two, one."

L'owuro started to drift away from the asteroid when Adejola finished his countdown.

"Set an intercept course for *Ebun* and engage at maximum."

"Course laid in, sir," Adejola said.

"Full scan," Tobi said to Ama.

"Regret to inform the war chief that *Ebun* has been modified with a scan-resistant hull. We cannot get solid readings of the ship's interior."

Tobi pounded the arm of his command chair. He should have expected such a modification, and he made a mental note to punch Hembadoon in the nose at the earliest opportunity.

"Engaging course," Adejola said. "ETA in three minutes."

Tobi frowned. If *L'owuro* moving at maximum cut the ETA that much, *Ebun* couldn't have been moving very quickly.

As if reading his mind, Ama said, "Picking up one odd reading, sir."

She hesitated, prompting Tobi to turn and glower at her. "Well?"

"Uhm, well, the ships the Orisha use have dual Sogba engines."

"Cavalry Master, my interest in the minutiae of engineering is all but nonexistent."

"My point, sir," Ama said quickly, "is that, as far as I can tell, only one of the engines is working. The ship may be damaged, sir."

"Full tac alert," Tobi said. "She may be damaged, or the Ori-Inu may want us to think she's damaged so we'll get cocky." He turned back around to face the forward viewer. "Pretending you're more hurt than you are to lure your foe into a false sense of security may be the oldest trick in the book, but that's because it still works. Proceed with caution, Cavalry Chief."

"Yes, sir."

It wasn't until they were within docking range that the cavalryman at communications said, "Sir, we're receiving a disaster beacon from *Ebun*—Code 47."

Ama said, "What? But nothing's changed. Why wait until now to—"

And then Tobi realized what Folami had done.

Leaping to his feet, Tobi cried, "Reverse course, Adejola, *now*! Before—"

The lights on the flight deck all suddenly went red, and a three-beat klaxon started going off.

"*Mogbe*," Tobi muttered.

"I've lost helm control!" Adejola said.

"My board's down," Ama added.

The comm officer said, "I can't get a response from my console, either—but we are getting an incoming call from *Ebun*."

A recorded voice sounded over the speakers. "Attention— your vessel has been commandeered by an Orisha for a Code 47 emergency. Please do not be alarmed. The Orisha will communicate with you shortly."

Tobi shook his head. "Gotta give the little *buruku* credit—she really *is* that good. *Ebun* will hold us until there's instructions from Hembadoon—who won't be giving any from the medical quarters on Olokun."

"Sir, we have to prepare for boarding. She probably did this to cripple us so she could take over the ship."

"Hm?" Tobi turned to look at Ama. "All right, go ahead and do so on the off-chance that I'm wrong, but the Ori-Inu isn't on that ship and won't be on this one."

"Sir?" Ama sounded confused.

The war chief sat back down in his chair, wishing he'd brought his brandy bottle to the flight deck with him. "She wants to stop Ojiji, Cavalry Master. This was just a diversion to get *L'owuro* away from the asteroid. Olokun's her target."

Then he got back up. There was nothing he could do here in any case. "Cavalry Master, I want this ship back under our control as soon as humanly possible, if not sooner. The faster it's done, the less likely you'll be busted down to cavalrywoman, am I clear?"

"Yes, *sir*," Ama said.

"Good. I'll be in my cabin."

FOURTEEN
Olokun Station

ORANMIYAN KNEW THAT THE WHOLE thing was just totally completely thoroughly utterly messed up.

He had to do something about that.

Yes, yes, yes he did.

He had to stop everything from going totally completely thoroughly utterly wrong.

Abeje would be able to help. That was why he wanted Abeje along, because he knew that she would be running the program, right by his side with them together just like it was back during training, when it was her and him and Folami and they were Hembadoon's best trainees and they were going to be the best of the best of the best of the best.

(Abeje's dead.)

No, Abeje wasn't dead. Abeje was helping him.

(She's dead.)

It wasn't supposed to be this way.

When he was growing up in the slums of Benin, he had thought he knew how life was going to go. Grandma tried to raise him her way, but he didn't have any truck with her voodoo nonsense. It got her through the day, and that was just fine, but Oranmiyan didn't have anything to do with that foolishness.

Grandma was respected, so people left her alone. In his neighborhood, that was huge. It was everyone for themselves there, and if you didn't protect yourself, you were doomed.

The way Grandma protected herself was to serve the community. People didn't have much to believe in, so she gave them something.

It was all messed up, but Oranmiyan didn't care. It kept Grandma alive.

(Grandma's dead, too.)

Oranmiyan's way of getting through the day was to be bigger and smarter than everyone. Either one by itself would've been fine, but he was both. Nobody pissed him off, and nobody did anything to him.

It was when Hembadoon showed up that he realized he was a telepath. He told him what he was and what he could do. He was to become an Ori-Inu, fight the good fight. He believed in the program, believed in using his abilities to make the system a better place for everyone.

The training with Hembadoon with Folami and Abeje— those were the best times. Sure, there were problems here and there, but they were the best of the best of the best of the best of the best of the best.

He lead them. He and Abeje and Folami.

(Abeje is dead.)

Everything was great.

At least until that crazy Eso super-soldier.

(Yeah, and he's dead, too.)

(Everyone's dead.)

(Except Folami.)

The Eso super-soldier didn't just make him unreadable.

The Eso super-soldier didn't just make him immune to

mindwiping (which he didn't tell anybody).

The Eso super-soldier opened his eyes.

The Eso super-soldier made him free.

Not that he was thankful or anything. The Eso and the Oyo rebels they slaved for were a blot on the universe, the final convulsions of an empire that was already dead, and Oranmiyan had taken pleasure every single time he killed one of them.

But they made him free.

Free to see the Hegemony for what it was.

Free to see what they were doing to telepaths like him and Folami and Abeje and all the rest of them.

(Abeje's dead.)

(You killed her.)

(You broke her neck.)

He couldn't convince them that they were wrong, though, because their program was written, and he couldn't override.

So he faked his own death. He left his comrades, his friends, behind. But he swore that one day he would rescue them.

(You're not dead.)

And then he met Tobi.

(He lied to you.)

That *buruku* Tobi.

That murderous *buruku* Tobi.

That murderous lying *buruku* Tobi.

(He's still alive.)

No! No, Tobi introduced him to Shango-oti. Showed him how psis could be more than just the limited Ori-Inu that the Hegemony turned out.

Oranmiyan was more powerful now.

He could take on anybody.

Kill anybody.

(Like Abeje.)

No! Abeje wasn't dead!

(Yes, she is. You killed her.)

"Noooooooooooooo!"

"I *said* stand down, Oranmiyan! Orders from the war chief!"

Oranmiyan looked around. He had no idea where the three armored personnel had come from.

(They're from Rufiji Company.)

All three of them were pointing their weapons at Oranmiyan.

If he hadn't been so distracted by his worries that everything was going to hell, he would've noticed.

But now he was surrounded.

One-point-five seconds later, he was no longer surrounded.

The cavalry chief died imagining the look of surprise on his wife's face when he pointed his Bayo pistol at her and her lover. The cavalrywoman died wishing her father would leave her alone. The cavalryman died wondering what would be for dinner tonight.

They all lay on the floor of Olokun Station, blood oozing out of their eyes, ears, and noses.

Oranmiyan didn't give the three people he'd killed a second thought. He had to find Abeje.

(Abeje is dead.)

No! He just had to find her.

(You killed her.)

He ran toward the lab.

Folami hadn't been prepared for so much *emptiness*.

Her plan had been a simple one: bring *Ebun* to a spot that was far enough away from Olokun Station that *L'owuro* would need to disengage from the station to investigate. She'd use the

Ori-Inu priority—that blessed authority that Oba Isembi had said was in full effect for this mission—to trap the cavalry vessel for as long as it would take *L'owuro*'s techs to work around it.

But by the time *L'owuro* arrived, Folami would be long gone. Because neither *L'owuro* nor War Chief Tobi was her target.

The heart of Ojiji was Olokun Station, and Folami was determined to destroy it.

She put on the EVA suit, made sure the air supply was filled and functioning, likewise the thrusters, and armed herself with the two grenades and three guns. Then she used *Ebun*'s computer to calculate the trajectory required for her plan.

Once the ship was in place, and the program to neutralize *L'owuro* put on standby pending the ship's arrival, Folami stood in the exact spot in the depressurized airlock that the computer dictated, and kicked off from *Ebun*. Once she was clear of the ship, she activated the thrusters, which shot her off directly at one of Olokun Station's two emergency airlocks, at a speed that would get her there in two hours.

Thus far, the plan had worked. She was able to hear the thoughts of Tobi and his crew as they traveled from the modified asteroid to *Ebun*'s location. She herself was too small to register on their scanners unless they were specifically looking for her.

She also felt the frustration of the crew as the Ori-Inu priority program she'd initiated crippled *L'owuro* pending instructions from an Orisha—instructions that would, of course, never come.

But from Tobi, she only felt his usual bland affect. Only now did she know that his preternatural calm was a façade, one that she was unable to penetrate. She wondered how powerful he really was.

As she flew unfettered through the vacuum of space, she

found herself overwhelmed by how *empty* everything was. There was literally nothing around her. All her other trips through space were done in ships, mostly surrounded by other people, and her previous EVA experiences were all proximate to ships, planets, and/or stations. There was always *something* nearby, some point of reference.

But soon enough, both *Ebun* and *L'owuro* were too far away to be anything other than a small point in the distance, indistinguishable from hundreds of other small points. Olokun was the same. And she was too distant to sense the thoughts of anyone on *L'owuro* or in Olokun.

She was alone.

With a start, Folami realized that she'd never truly been alone like this in her life.

There were no other thoughts nearby.

A huge smile broke out on her face.

Absolute quiet. So this is what it's like!

The smile expanded into a laugh. She laughed so hard that she feared she would send her suit off course—a potentially fatal occurrence, as a course alteration of just half a degree would send her careening into space where she'd get to enjoy the quiet for a great deal longer.

Folami was *happy*. She hadn't been this filled with joy since the night of her tenth birthday party. That was her last happy day before her parents sent her to Olorun.

Then she started to sense the thoughts of the people in Olokun Station, and she screamed out loud, "No!" Her hands reached out to grab something that would make her stop her forward motion, but the same emptiness that had embraced her was now denying her, keeping her from her bliss.

The thoughts became clearer as she got closer—nothing too

distinguishable, nobody she recognized, but the definite feel of people.

Ever so slowly, the point in front of her enlarged until it was obviously an asteroid. And ever so slowly, her joy dissipated.

And ever so slowly, her desire to destroy Ojiji intensified. That was twice now that they had restored her misery after she had set it aside.

Once she got within a kilometer or so of the asteroid, she flipped herself over so that her feet faced the station, and fired the boot thrusters again, this time to slow herself down.

When her velocity was down to almost nothing, she let herself drift gently onto the rocky surface of the asteroid. The station had rotated more than she'd realized, and was several meters from the emergency airlock that she had been aiming for.

That was only a minor inconvenience, though. The fingers and palms of the gloves and the balls, heels, and fronts of the boots of the EVA suits could adhere to most surfaces. She was easily able to clamber across the rock until she reached the solid metal door of the emergency airlock, which had a keypad next to it, both embedded in the rock.

On a whim, she attempted to enter her Ori-Inu code. The display over the keypad lit up with the words **access denied**.

Didn't think that would work, she thought as she attached one of the grenades to the door, set the timer for one minute, then clambered back along the asteroid. She moved farther than she needed to—the grenades provided a shaped charge that would blow outward, so she really only needed to move a meter to the side of the door to be safe. But it was better to err on the side of caution.

After one minute, the grenade blew with a flash of light and a sudden spread of metal fragments and quickly freezing dust particles and air into space.

If Olokun used the same protocols as Hegemony ships and bases, the airlock inner door would now be shut and would remain so until security gave the all-clear. Before that would happen, a damage-control team would be scrambled to assess the damage. Since this airlock was useless, they would have to come through a different egress. Folami figured it would be at least seven minutes before they would be anywhere nearby.

She'd done no active psionic work since she left *L'owuro*, and had eaten and drunk and gotten lots of rest, so she figured to be at full capacity.

Which was good, as her next trick was going to be tough.

Moving back to the now-shattered airlock door, she saw the small interior, with another keypad next to the inner door. The display over that keypad read **emergency lockdown**.

Not for long, Folami thought with a smile.

Taking a few deep breaths for good measure, and *not* twitching her nose, she both opened the airlock door and held the air on the other side from moving.

As a general rule, molecules moved from an area of greater concentration to one of lesser concentration. That most basic of natural laws led to explosive decompression when a sealed environment in a vacuum had a breach.

Right now, only Folami's will kept the air molecules inside the station after the door opened.

The hardest part, though, was to move through her own self-imposed barricade and enter the atmosphere of the station proper. A spike of pain drove through her right eye as she willed the airlock door open and the air not to move even though her own body was displacing it.

Once she got through, she released the door, which slid quickly shut.

Then she collapsed against the wall.

Ceasing her hold on the door and air had done little to relieve the pain behind her eye. Pausing to catch her breath, she then broke the seal on her helmet and removed it.

Depressingly, the air in the station was just as stale as it had become in her suit.

After wiping the blood from her upper lip with the sleeve of her EVA suit, she removed the suit, then activated its security system. Now if anyone other than herself or Hembadoon touched the suit, it would explode, likely killing anyone in a one-meter radius.

Under the EVA suit, she wore a long leather coat that Hembadoon had in a storage compartment on *Ebun*. The coat had heating circuitry woven inside it, probably meant for use during planetary winters—or any time he visited Esu. It was only marginally more protection than that provided by the hospital gown, but she took what she could get.

She started moving through the station, an Ayoka rifle in each hand, with the Bayo pistol in the coat's right pocket, the remaining grenade now in the left pocket.

Reaching out with her mind, she tried to find the familiar thoughts of either Abeje or Hembadoon.

She couldn't sense Abeje at all, but Hembadoon's mind was quite clear—and agitated.

Closer to her current location, though, was a highly powerful telepath. *A Nide coming to play.*

His thoughts were wild and chaotic and hard to pin down, but she got his name: Alagbara. She recalled that he was among the missing Ori-Inu, and that she'd gone on a mission with him once.

He also wasn't looking for her, but was trying to avoid Cavalry Master Apara.

When Folami rounded a corner, he was standing waiting for her, wearing white armor, a wrist weapon pointed at her. She immediately tried to telekinetically fire her Ayokas—

—then screamed in pain as agony sliced into her skull. It was the worst pain she'd felt since she destroyed Yemoja.

"Ha! See there, Folami? See, we were ready for you this time, Folami. Ready to do business and not get put in a box, ain't that right, Folami? No more of your *oluwa*, always getting the good assignments. Precious tenth-level *buruku*. Well, that ain't no good to you now, Folami, 'cause what we got here is feedback that only affects ninth-levels or higher if they do anything. Know what that means? Means you can't do anything. Not without a world of pain, anyhow. So, Folami, you got anything to say?"

In fact, Folami had nothing to say, but was happy to take advantage of Alagbara's gloating to focus past the pain and strike back, mindblasting what passed for his brain into mulch.

Staring down at the corpse inside the armor that was now hemorrhaging blood from his eyes, nose, ears, and mouth, she said, "I've been living with a lot more than a world of pain for years now, you stupid *buruku*."

Then she shot him repeatedly with the Ayokas. Eventually, the pain stopped, meaning that her rounds had destroyed the device causing the feedback.

Folami considered then abandoned the notion of trying to put on one of the Nide suits of armor. If Tobi and Oranmiyan had any sense, they'd be biometrically keyed to the user, same as the Ori-Inu armor.

She sensed four cavalry on their way toward her from the other direction, so she kept moving forward, hoping to stay ahead of them. After all that, she really needed to conserve her energy.

Interestingly, the cavalry weren't after her, but were looking for Alagbara.

When she turned a corner, she literally bumped into Oranmiyan.

To her shock and disgust, he was holding Abeje in his arms—and she was dead.

"Folami? It's you! Good! Now it can be like it was, you know? It's all good now. All good. Yes, it is."

Folami blinked. Oranmiyan's eyes were glazed, his tone was softer than usual, and he barely seemed aware of the corpse in his arms.

Oh mogbe, *he has lost it.* "Oranmiyan? What happened to Abeje?"

"Nothing. We're all together again, that's all, just like it was in the good old times. Remember those good times with Orisha Hembadoon? Those were some *good* times."

Folami felt that the four cavalry were now almost upon them. Oranmiyan's apparent descent into madness brought her up short. She had been prepared to fight him, not see him broken like this.

One of the cavalry said, "Both of you, stand very still and put your hands where I can see them."

Folami ignored him, instead staring at Oranmiyan.

"It's fine, Cavalryman," Oranmiyan muttered. "Everything's taken care of."

"I'm sorry, Oranmiyan," the cavalryman said, "but I have orders straight from War Chief Tobi to take both of you to detention until *L'owuro* returns—and also to dispose of Abeje's corpse."

That was the wrong thing to say. Oranmiyan's face exploded into blind fury. "Shut up! Shut up! She's not dead, dammit, shut *up!*"

Suddenly, Folami found herself on her knees, her headache having intensified a hundredfold. *I would kill for my armor right now, just for the supply of analgesics,* she thought, wondering how and when her knees buckled.

She also didn't sense any active minds nearby. Looking behind her, she saw that all four cavalry were dead.

"Oranmiyan?" she said slowly, getting to her feet.

He was caressing Abeje's face now. Folami could see that her friend's neck had been broken, and she wondered how it happened.

She had a horrible feeling as to what the answer was—which may have had as much to do with Oranmiyan's instability as the Shango-oti.

"Come on, Folami," he finally said, "let's go to the hangar. We can get away."

"I can't leave, Oranmiyan," she said. "This place—it has to be destroyed. Ojiji is an abomination."

"No!" he screamed, dropping Abeje's body to the ground. "You don't understand—Shango-oti, it'll make you *free!*"

"Free to do *what*? Oranmiyan, you remember me during training? You remember how desperately, more than anything else, I wanted to *forget who I was*? All the death and destruction, all the people that Olorun made me kill! When I was exposed to your filthy Shango-oti, it undid *all* of the mindwiping! I remember *every single person* that I killed, Oranmiyan! All the people on Yemoja—it's more than I can bear, and I'll be *damned* if I let that happen to anyone else!"

Even as she was screaming, Folami felt the presence of four more cavalry coming down the corridor. The pounding in her head was a warning to go easy on the telepathy, so instead she raised her weapons.

That was a mistake, as Oranmiyan seemed to assume she was pointing her Ayokas at him. *How far gone is he?*

And how far gone am I?

She telekinetically shoved Oranmiyan out of her way, even as he was about to fire his own Ayoka. His rounds fired into the ceiling as he fell.

Folami fired both weapons, which tore through the armor of each cavalry as they rounded the corner, before they'd even had a chance to get Folami in their sights.

As she shot them, she heard the orders that all four of them had received directly from Tobi, still stuck on *L'owuro* in Folami's trap: *"Your orders are to kill both Folami and Oranmiyan. She's too dangerous and he's become too much of a liability. Use any means necessary."*

"Dammit, Folami, why are you doing this? We can be free and together again just like the old days and we'll be free!"

"We weren't 'free' in the old days, Oranmiyan, we were under the Hegemony's thumb. They mindwiped us every other day to cover things up!"

"I know that!" he cried. "But it's different now!"

"How?" Folami pointed at Abeje's corpse. "How is that different? What did Abeje do to deserve that?"

Oranmiyan stared down at Abeje's corpse.

"No, it's not like that." He knelt down and held Abeje's broken body against his massive chest. "It'll all be okay. Shango-oti will—"

"All Shango-oti will do is trade Isembi for Tobi. Come *on*, Oranmiyan, you can read these guys as well as I can. Tobi wants us *both* dead, because we're both messing with his plan."

"No!" Oranmiyan screamed, and Folami felt his scream in her mind even more than she heard it with her ears. One massive fist careened toward Folami's head with the same speed as that of the Eso on Oshun, and she was barely able to mentally shove it aside the same way.

"It's not like that! It's all gonna be good, like it used to be!"

Folami considered then abandoned the notion of trying to convince Oranmiyan that their days as trainees were far from an ideal time to be re-created—especially since he himself faked his own death to get away from it. Rational arguments weren't going to win the day here.

Instead, she blew out the rock wall next to Oranmiyan.

In Kaduna Township, an attempt to do something similar with the cornice Oranmiyan was standing behind failed because Oranmiyan saw it coming.

On Olokun Station, though, Oranmiyan didn't even notice that Folami hadn't wrinkled her nose this time.

Screaming with pain as the rocks sliced into his large forearms—he wasn't so far gone that he didn't know to raise his arms to protect his face—Folami didn't wait for him to recover, instead leaping toward him with a jumping side kick to the solar plexus.

She regretted the action as soon as her bare foot struck Oranmiyan's rock-hard stomach. She'd been unable to use her telekinesis to make the kick stronger—too much psionics in too short a time—and without the heavy-soled boots of her battlesuit, her foot took the brunt of the impact.

However, Oranmiyan did stumble backward even as Folami fell to the floor.

Pushing herself to her feet, Folami said, "It's over, Oranmiyan. All of it."

But Oranmiyan wasn't getting up. Instead, he rocked back and forth on the floor, blood dripping from his arms, muttering to himself.

"It'll be good again, just like the old days, all of us together again, just like the old days, it'll all be good again, you'll see, me, Folami, Abeje, the best of the best of the best of the best, we'll show them, we will . . ."

Folami stared down at the man who she once considered her closest friend, and thought about how much she had lost.

And how much she never had.

There was little she could do for Oranmiyan, and less she could do for Abeje.

But I can end this project once and for all.

Promising herself that she'd come back for Oranmiyan and for Abeje's body—no matter what happened, she owed both of them that—she ran toward the inner section of the asteroid. From the wounded and dying security personnel, Folami had telepathically gleaned the precise layout of Olokun Station, and discerned where they were holding Hembadoon. That was her next stop.

As she ran through the rocky corridors, which were even harsher than the metal decks of *L'owuro* on her bare feet, she soon came across two more corpses, both bleeding from the eyes, nose, ears, and mouth.

Oranmiyan must have done this.

There were only eight other cavalry still left on the station—Olokun's primary security was secrecy, after all—and they were occupied gathering up the remaining Nide and the support staff. Interestingly, the Nide were being placed into stasis pods. Some of them were even going willingly. *Probably a security precaution—Tobi doesn't want any telepaths sensing the Nide on L'owuro.*

Tobi was planning to abandon Olokun Station. Folami wasn't letting him get away that easily.

Thanks to the reduced security being so fully occupied, Folami didn't encounter anybody by the time she reached the room where Hembadoon was being held.

Conveniently, both the people she wanted to find were present: Hembadoon and Cavalry Master Apara. There was a third, Doctor Ogumefu. Apara's thoughts were urgent, Ogumefu's frustrated, Hembadoon's angry.

Holding back for a moment, Folami telepathically eavesdropped on the conversation in the room, which also gave her a moment to learn the layout, and where everyone was. Hembadoon was lying on a pallet in restraints, with Ogumefu standing nearby, looking at something on a computer screen. Apara was standing about a meter behind Ogumefu.

"Doc, will you hurry up?" Apara was saying, anxiously. Her primary concern was to get Ogumefu and Hembadoon to the airlock so they could board *L'owuro* when it came back.

Which was sooner than Folami had expected. She had been hoping to get another hour or so, but Tobi's techs were obviously better than she thought. She read in Apara's mind that *L'owuro's* ETA was ten minutes.

"Just one second, please," Ogumefu said in clipped tones. He was anxious, too, but it was the excitement of a scientific discovery. "I'm just getting the results of the subject's DNA scan, and it's fascinating."

"It can also be fascinating on *L'owuro*, Doc. We need to go, now. You can poke and prod him some more later."

Apara's urgency was borne of the *other* duty she had. Once she got Ogumefu and Hembadoon to the airlock, she was to go to the security office and start the destruction sequence. Her orders were to time it for ten minutes after *L'owuro* was fully loaded and away from the asteroid.

Folami smiled. This made her plan easier to enact.

"Yes, yes, of course," Ogumefu said, distractedly.

Then Folami's smile fell. Ogumefu's thoughts regarding "the subject" made Folami ill. The doctor was frustrated by Tobi's insistence on keeping Hembadoon alive, as Ogumefu felt he could learn so much more from dissecting the Orisha.

Scanning further into Ogumefu's mind revealed even more—including both dissection and vivisection of certain Nide. Some were Ori-Inu that Folami knew and had worked with.

Knowing that made her next move much easier. Psionically taking aim before she even came inside, she entered the room and shot Ogumefu four times in the chest with one of her stolen Ayokas, the first round pulverizing his heart before she even saw him.

Her only regret was that he never saw the kill shot coming, and so died without being aware of who killed him.

Folami regretted that. And a moment later, she regretted that it had come to this: she *enjoyed* killing someone.

Those thoughts passed through her mind in an instant. The other Ayoka was trained on Apara's left knee.

Apara had been holding her own Ayoka at her chest, so pointing it at Folami would only have taken a second, but Folami didn't give her that second.

"Don't move, Apara," she said for good measure.

From the pallet came a chuckle. "About time you showed up."

Sparing a glance at Hembadoon, she saw that he was smiling raggedly. "Sorry—had to get Tobi out of the way. Oh, and I ate all of your food. *Don't* move, Apara," she added when she sensed that Apara tightened her grip on her Ayoka. "You know damn well what I am—you saw plenty of it on Oshun when I saved you all from the Eso. I know when you move, I know when you blink, and I know that you want to live long enough so that your next payday will cover the last of your uncle's medical expenses. Oh, and if you fire, I'll make your Ayoka blow up in your face."

As she said these words to Apara, she kept her left arm in the same place relative to Apara's knee, even as she moved toward the pallet and released Hembadoon. At no point did she actually look at Apara.

The moment his hands were free, Hembadoon yanked the psionic blocker off his forehead. "Finally!"

Only then did Folami turn to make eye contact with Apara. "Now then—you have orders from War Chief Tobi to set the destruction sequence. We're going to go do that, just on a slightly faster timetable."

"No chance, Ori-Inu. *I'm* the only one authorized to activate that sequence—not even Tobi can do it. Which means you can't kill me."

Folami sighed. She'd been hoping to do this the easy way.

"You're right," she said to Apara, "I can't kill you."

Then she shot Apara in the knee.

"Yeearrrrrrrrrrrh!" Apara collapsed to the floor, her Ayoka clattering on the rock.

Hembadoon smoothly picked the weapon up, while Folami

removed Apara's helmet, and then locked eyes with the woman and concentrated.

While Hembadoon provided most of her training, he sometimes had to leave to find and recruit more telepaths. During those periods, others would come in to teach, and one such was an Ori-Inu named Aiku. He had taught her mind-control. It was incredibly difficult to accomplish, especially with a subject who was either unconscious or asleep—because the body resisted control when it was shut down like that—or fully conscious and actively resisting.

The easiest person to control was a conscious subject who was in pain. The victim was unable to focus on much beyond agony. And Hembadoon had always said that knees were the best place to injure someone you didn't want to kill, as it caused the greatest amount of pain with the least likelihood of dying.

The trick was to slowly move through the victim's mind and find the higher nerve functions. All you *really* needed to have control of were the arms and legs. Aiku had also instructed her never to bother with controlling the victim's voice, unless it was absolutely necessary (say, for purposes of deceiving someone), as it was a great deal of trouble to match speaking patterns, and if the victim could talk, they usually wasted energy on doing so rather than on fighting back.

On this particular occasion, Folami had the added distraction of the drill behind her eyes going back on full. She hadn't given herself adequate time to recover from holding the air in at the airlock and fighting through Alagbara's feedback, so holding onto Apara was going to be difficult.

Folami's first question for Aiku had been why she couldn't just manipulate a subject telekinetically. The teacher had replied that it was possible, but it took considerably more effort to so precisely manipulate a person's body to move smoothly. Doing that to a body meant that that body moved awkwardly. He even had Folami try it with a volunteer subject, who moved in a herky-jerky fashion, falling over several times.

But when she had controlled that same volunteer's nervous sytem—controlling, as Aiku had put it, from the inside rather than the outside—he had walked naturally and gracefully.

Without looking at Hembadoon, she reached out to hand him one of her weapons. "Take this."

Hembadoon took the Ayoka, now holding one in each hand.

Apara, predictably, was wasting energy talking. Her voice was halting, and through clenched teeth, as she still felt every bit of the pain of her shattered knee. "You're never—never gonna get—get away with this, you stupid—stupid *buruku*."

Folami ignored her. "Hembadoon, I need you to cover me while we go to the security office."

"No problem."

"And you'd better get in touch with *Ebun*. It's in-system."

"Way ahead of you—first thing I did when I got that thing off my head was to call her back."

Another trick Aiku had taught her was to coordinate your own movements with that of the victim. It saved the difficulty of splitting your focus. It wasn't always practical to do so, but now it worked out nicely. Folami fell into step behind Apara, the cavalry master's enforced steps matching those of Folami as they left the room and moved into the corridor. Hembadoon took up the rear position, guarding Folami's back.

It took all of Folami's concentration to maintain her hold on Apara, so she was unable to keep a psionic eye out for the rest of the base. She had to count on Hembadoon to protect her in case a Nide or someone from security came by.

While no one did intercept them, there were two cavalry in the office itself. Folami only found this out when Apara demonstrated the disadvantage of leaving the victim control of her vocal cords.

"Cavalrymen, fire, now!"

Folami barely registered the two before they fired their Ayokas.

But the rounds stopped in midair and then fell to the floor, harmless.

Hembadoon smiled. "Orisha robes come with a force field."

Then he fired both of his Ayokas at the two shocked guards, who stumbled backwards from the impact, which also damaged their armor.

"Looks like yours doesn't. I'd talk to the manufacturer."

The cavalrymen fired again, still to no effect.

Hembadoon then fired again, and kept firing his Ayokas on automatic until the armor of both guards was shredded.

Folami wanted to feel remorse at the deaths of these two. They were just cavalry following orders and doing their duty.

But just the fact that they served under Tobi kept Folami from feeling any sympathy.

And that just made her more determined to destroy Ojiji.

"You filthy *buruku*," Apara said breathlessly and drowsily. The pain was starting to take its toll, and if the cavalry master was to remain conscious long enough to do what Folami needed her to do, she needed to move quickly.

She had Apara walk to the computer console (stepping over the corpses as she did so) and press her left hand to the scanner that would identify her biometrics.

Once the computer screen showed a status message acknowledging that this was indeed Cavalry Master Apara,

Folami had her type in the instructions to activate the destruction sequence.

"*L'owuro* to Cavalry Master Apara. We've docked with Olokun. The war chief's requesting a status report."

"*Mogbe*," Apara said. Without the ability to move her hands, she couldn't activate an intercom—either on the console or on her suit of armor—to reply.

Folami shared her sentiment for different reasons. Once *L'owuro* realized that Apara couldn't report in, Tobi would know that she was compromised.

"How close is *Ebun*?" she asked Hembadoon.

"It'll be docked with the emergency airlock in seven minutes."

Nodding, Folami had Apara set the destruction sequence for fifteen minutes.

"That's that," Folami said. "Let's get to—"

Apara interrupted. "You're never—gonna get—get off this rock—alive."

Before Folami could say anything, Hembadoon said, "Yes, well, neither are you," prior to firing both Ayokas at her unprotected head.

Once again, Folami wanted to feel remorse at another death that she was responsible for, even if indirectly. Once again, she couldn't.

She looked at Hembadoon, who looked back at her with great sadness. "I'm sorry, Folami, but there was no way we could—"

Holding up a hand, she said, "No, you're right, Hembadoon. It's— Never mind. Let's get to the airlock."

Leaving three more corpses in her wake, Folami and Hembadoon ran toward the airlock.

When they got to where she'd left Oranmiyan and the bodies of Abeje and the cavalry, she found only the latter. Oranmiyan had gone and taken Abeje's body with him.

Options flew by in her mind, but she was forced to reject all but one: leave them behind. *Ebun* could only fit two. She couldn't read Oranmiyan, so finding him psionically was impossible, and without her armor, she couldn't seek him out that way.

Of course, Hembadoon's suit worked just fine, but then they came back to the lack of room in *Ebun*—not to mention a rapidly dwindling time frame before Olokun Station blew up.

I'm sorry, Abeje. I wanted to at least give you a proper burial. You deserved that much.

I'm sorry, Oranmiyan. I wanted to help you.

Putting her regrets aside, she kept running alongside Hembadoon toward the airlock.

FIFTEEN
L'owuro

ADEJOLA STOOD NEAR THE *L'OWURO* airlock, trying to figure out the best way to approach War Chief Tobi.

He'd rehearsed and rejected any number of openings to the conversation, knowing that the wrong thing was likely to get him killed.

Like most of *L'owuro*'s officer corps, Adejola knew about Ojiji. Adejola had been in favor of Tobi's attempted *coup* simply because he was incredibly disappointed with the *coup*'s intended target. Adejola had hope that Tobi's regime would *truly* be a change for the better.

Given what he'd been seeing for the past day, he was no longer quite so sure of that. He'd asked Folami out on a date because he genuinely liked her, and he figured she'd be recruited for Ojiji soon enough, so they'd get to see a great deal of each other. But then Tobi told her that she'd need "convincing," and that he'd be putting her in the brig "for her own good."

So when Folami came to his cabin, Adejola had been surprised. And also concerned.

It had taken every ounce of will power Adejola had to not finish what he and Folami started. Had Tobi not told him of his plans, he would have, but knowing that Folami was supposed to be anaesthetized in her own cabin forced him to contact Tobi.

He was too good an officer to do otherwise.

But a good officer also questioned orders if they were sufficiently outrageous, and what he'd seen since they left Oshun indicated that Tobi was going to kill Folami and Oranmiyan both.

While Tobi had recruited Adejola when he requested that the pilot transfer to *L'owuro*, it was Oranmiyan who had convinced him that Ojiji was a worthwhile endeavor, that it would free the Ori-Inu from their servitude to Isembi and allow them their freedom.

Reality was proving rather different.

Tobi, dressed in his full armor, but without his helmet, came stomping down the corridor toward the airlock with Cavalry Master Morayo and three other cavalry in tow.

"Excuse me, War Chief Tobi?"

"I don't have time to talk to you, Cavalryman."

"Er, it's Cavalry Chief, sir, and—"

Tobi glared at him. "It's going to *be* 'Cavalryman' if you don't shut up and get out of my way, Adejola, am I understood?"

"Sir, it's important. I don't think you should give up on Folami so easily."

Tobi then did the most frightening thing Adejola had ever seen the war chief do in all his time serving under him: he laughed.

Swallowing, Adejola said, "Sir, I'm sorry, but I'm not joking."

The laugh stopped, the glare coming back full force. "Neither am I, Cavalry Chief. Folami has proven intractable. She is dedicated to destroying Ojiji, and has done nothing since learning of the project save try to eliminate it. And we've all seen how good she is at accomplishing what she sets out to do.

Therefore she has to die. Now I'm sorry if this interferes with your sex life, but so be it."

Even as Adejola realized that this was a lost cause, even as he thought to himself that it was all over, he heard himself speak without thinking: "Let me talk to her."

Tobi blinked, and Adejola took some small comfort in the fact that he shocked the war chief—not an easy task. "Excuse me, Cavalry Chief?"

"Let me talk to her. I think I can get through to her."

This prompted yet another laugh from Tobi, which was louder, sharper, and nastier than the first. "So let me see if I understand you, Cavalry Chief. You think that you can get through to the Ori-Inu. You think that you have won the trust of a young woman who came to your cabin in the hopes of an amorous encounter, during which you set her up to be captured by a project that she has dedicated herself to destroying. You truly think this?"

It sounded better in Adejola's head, though he did not say that aloud. "It's—it's not likely, I admit, sir, but— Well, sir, what do you have to lose? You yourself have said several times that Folami would be an asset to the program."

Tobi put a hand to his chin.

"All right, Cavalry Chief—let's give it a shot."

Now it was Adejola's turn to be surprised. "Really, sir?"

Unholstering his Bayo and pointing it at Adejola's head, Tobi said, "No, not really."

The last thing Adejola heard was the pistol's report before it blew his brains out.

Tobi shook his head as he looked down at the near-headless corpse of Cavalry Chief Adejola. *What an imbecile.*

That was the last thought he gave to Adejola.

Activating the airlock, he walked through it once it was fully pressurized and entered Olokun Station, Morayo and the other three cavalry trailing behind him.

However, as soon as he did so, he saw several red lights blinking in sequence. That meant that the destruction sequence—which Apara wasn't supposed to even start until *L'owuro* was fully loaded—had already commenced.

Turning around, he said, "Cavalry Master Morayo, interface with the Olokun computer—status report."

Were he wearing his helmet, he could do likewise, but the helmet interfered with his ability to use his psionics. Normally that wasn't an issue, but against Folami, he was going to need every edge he could get. She had a higher rating than he did—Tobi wasn't sure what his own level was, as such things hadn't been formalized until after he'd gone off the grid as a psi, but Tobi's lack of telekinesis meant he had to be at a number lower than Folami's ten—but Tobi had far more experience.

His experience had always allowed him to win. That, and using the right tools for the job. Currently, one of those tools was his armor, which was pumping Shango-oti directly into his blood stream. Hell, maybe he'd be a tenth-level like that stupid little *buruku* soon enough.

Anxiously, Morayo said, "Sir, the destruction sequence is active and set for twelve minutes, fifty seconds, and counting!"

"Mogbe." Tobi reached out with his mind, but could not find Apara. Folami must have killed her after getting her to start the sequence.

"Sir," Morayo added, "I'm only getting live readings in two locations—the stasis chamber and two unidentifieds moving through a rear corridor."

Reaching out with his mind, he read both Folami and Agent Hembadoon as the unidentifieds. "Cavalry Master, you have twelve minutes to evac everyone from the stasis chamber and get *L'owuro* away. Move!"

"Yes, sir!"

Even as Morayo led the other three cavalry toward the stasis chamber to rescue the remaining cavalry and the Nide—there were only six of the actives in suspended animation, which was less than Tobi had been hoping for—the war chief moved after Folami and Hembadoon.

While he could sense where Folami was, he couldn't read her thoughts—not even surface ones. *She's good. But so am I.*

He ran through the rocky corridors of Olokun Station. No way was Folami getting off this rock alive.

Just as he turned a corner to where he knew she was, the wall next to him shattered, sending shards of rock careening toward him. Tobi threw up his arms to protect his face, the armor getting the rest of it.

He projected his thoughts this time. *Nice try, Ori-Inu, but it won't work.*

The armor's autorepair kicked in as he rounded the corner and saw the most pathetic sight he'd ever expected to see.

Apparently, Folami hadn't had the opportunity to retrieve her red-and-black body armor. She stood alongside Hembadoon, facing Tobi in nothing but the hospital gown that Modupe's medtechs had put her in and a big leather coat.

He also saw the fatigue etched in Folami's face, the dried blood on her upper lip. She'd been straining herself. That would make Tobi's task easier.

Smiling, he said, "This is going to be more fun than I thought."

First, though, he had to get rid of the sidekick. With a quick thought, he mindblasted Hembadoon, using pure brute telepathic force to shut his mind down.

Except all Hembadoon did was wince and then fire with the Ayoka he was holding.

Forgot, he's an Orisha. Of course they have protection against psionic attack.

Tobi's armor continued to protect him, but he was regretting the decision to leave his helmet behind.

He fired his own Bayo at Hembadoon, but the Orisha's force field protected him.

Then Tobi heard Folami's thoughts, but they were directed at Hembadoon.

Hembadoon, we've only got ten minutes. You get to Ebun, I'll take care of Tobi.

Folami hadn't intended for Tobi to "overhear" that, but over the years, the war chief had learned the trick of tuning in to particular psionic signatures. He'd tuned into Folami's back when she first reported to *L'owuro,* and the Shango-oti had enhanced him enough that he could pick up her thoughts even when she was trying to keep them private.

Immediately, Tobi realized why they were back this way. Hembadoon's ship was at the nearby emergency airlock. The war chief used his suit's override to lock that airlock down so that only he could open it.

Letting Hembadoon go—Tobi decided that he wanted the Orisha to feel the frustration of being unable to get to his ship— he faced Folami. "That was a mistake, Ori-Inu. Two on one, you might have had a chance."

Folami stared at him with her obsidian eyes, which were bloodshot from all the psionic efforts she'd expended. "I don't need any help to kill you, War Chief."

"Better people than you have tried, Ori-Inu, and I'm still here."

What happened next happened quickly. Both Folami and Tobi tried to mindblast each other. It was a crude attack, but they were running out of time before Olokun would be destroyed.

The pair of them went back and forth. Folami's sheer psionic power made up for her fatigue, but Tobi could tell that she wasn't hitting him with her best shots, as his own defenses were good enough to prevent her from doing more than giving him a mild headache. He'd suffered worse from hangovers.

Folami's own defenses were good as well, and Tobi found he couldn't penetrate them.

So it's time for a more subtle attack.

One of Ojiji's recruits was a young woman with an amazing capacity for getting into computer records she wasn't supposed to. Tobi had found her in a Hegemony prison on Orunmila. Further proof, Tobi felt, that Isembi was an idiot. A leader with a brain in his head would have hired the woman on the spot to improve the security of the Hegemony's computer systems. Instead, Tobi arranged for her release and had her continue her work hacking Hegemony records until she died of a brain aneurysm a month earlier.

Thanks to her, though, Tobi knew everything about Folami.

So he used his training and the cover of their brute-force attacks on each other to worm his way into her mind . . .

Cavalry Master Morayo was the first one through the airlock door. She and the three cavalry with her had escorted the remains of the cavalry assigned to Olokun, the station staff, and the half-dozen stasis capsules containing the Nide to *L'owuro* in just enough time to get them on board before Olokun was destroyed.

Her armor's HUD told her that War Chief Tobi was still engaged with the Ori-Inu and the Orisha. That, frankly, suited Morayo just fine. She had gone along with the whole Ojiji program because the alternative was that that psychopath Tobi would have her killed. Besides, she had no great love for Oba Isembi.

But she had little love for Tobi, either, and even less when the *buruku* promoted that imbecile Apara over her to take over Rufiji.

With luck, the Ori-Inu and the war chief would kill each other. Two less freaks in the world *also* suited Morayo just fine.

As soon as she stepped through the airlock into *L'owuro*, and right when one of the cavalrymen had stepped into it, the door shut behind her.

Whirling around, Morayo cried, "What the hell?"

Over her helmet's intercom, the cavalryman who was actually in the airlock said, "Uh, Cavalry Master? The 'lock's cycling!"

"Flight deck, this is Morayo. Reopen airlock four, we need to evac the Nide from Olokun before it blows."

Silence met her query.

"Flight deck, this is Morayo, respond!"

"Cavalry Master?"

"Stand fast, Cavalryman, I'll get you out of there." She entered the override code on the airlock, but it didn't work.

L'owuro's engines were starting up—Morayo could feel the vibration through the deckplates even through her armored boots. Years of spaceship travel had taught her the signs, and she realized that some idiot on the flight deck was leaving Olokun too early.

"Flight deck," Morayo said as she entered the override code a fourth time to similar negative results, "you're about to condemn ten cavalry, six Nide, and a bunch of techs and support to death. Put the engines on standby and *reopen this airlock!*"

After a fifth entering of the override code, Morayo cursed and ran toward the front of the vessel, intending to personally shoot whoever was in command of the flight deck in the head.

"Cavalry Master?" came a very un-cavalry-like whimper through her intercom. "Don't leave me here, ma'am, please!"

Morayo cut the channel. She couldn't bear to listen to the poor man die.

As she beat feet down the corridor, she was struck by how empty it was. Usually there were always people walking the corridors—off-duty personnel wandering about, on-duty personnel going to duty stations or carrying things from one to another, and so on.

Then she saw the bodies.

Two engineers lay on the floor, bleeding from the eyes, nose, ears, and mouth. It was a particularly ugly death, one that Morayo had only seen a few times.

The more powerful Ori-Inu were able to kill people by mindblasting, which left a corpse like this.

But the Ori-Inu is with Tobi and all the Nide are in stasis. So who—?

Oh, mogbe.

Morayo started running down the corridor even as she activated her armor's HUD.

She only detected two life signs other than her own on board *L'owuro.* One was the cavalryman in airlock four. The other was on the flight deck.

There was nobody else alive on board the ship.

By the time Morayo made it to the flight deck, *L'owuro* had already disengaged from Olokun Station, and the number of life-sign readings was down to two. The cavalryman's body would float out in space—or, more likely, be blown to pieces when the asteroid exploded in less than three minutes.

Her Ayoka at the ready, Morayo stepped in front of the door, assuming it would read her biometrics and let her in.

It didn't.

So she shot the door repeatedly, blowing it to pieces. It took two dozen rounds, but eventually the Ayoka made a hole big enough for her to get through.

"You won't be killing me with that thing, Cavalry Master Morayo," said Oranmiyan from the command chair.

Morayo had never seen anyone other than Tobi sit in that chair since she reported to *L'owuro*, and it was a bizarre sight— made more so by the fact that Oranmiyan was cradling the corpse of one of the Nide in his arms, a sight that sickened her.

She also found that she couldn't move. Oranmiyan obviously had done one of his telepathy things to hold her still.

"I'll tell you the same thing I told Ama and the other officers, Cavalry Master. I'm taking *L'owuro*. It's mine now. You come with me, follow my orders, and we're solid."

"And if I tell you to die a horrible death?"

"Oh, I won't be the one dying."

Looking around the flight deck—Oranmiyan had only frozen her arms and legs—Morayo saw many more corpses beyond the Nide in Oranmiyan's lap. Cavalry Master Ama, and a dozen more officers and crew all lay sprawled over consoles and chairs and the deck. They all bled the same way the two engineers did.

Oranmiyan continued: "You got no loyalty to Tobi. I know that. So decide."

"You're a telepath," Morayo said. "You know my answer."

The last sounds Morayo would ever hear were Oranmiyan sighing and saying, "Yeah."

One moment, Folami was trying to wear down Tobi's psionic defenses.

The next, she was curled up in a corner of the small room in Olorun's sanctum where she slept.

Olorun was standing over her, smiling. It wasn't the friendly, pleasant smile on the holographs for the people of the Oyo Empire, no, this was a vicious, brutal, hateful smile.

For a moment, Folami feared that she was back on Yemoja, that everything that had happened to her in the years since her parents turned her over to their monarch had been a dream from which she had only just awakened.

But only for a moment.

Folami knew from dreams, and from nightmares. They were never this detailed.

To prove it, she grabbed Olorun and threw him against the wall.

"You're joking, right, War Chief?" she asked the air. "This is the best you can do?"

Then she was in the soccer stadium, the so-called enemies of the state—in truth, people who Olorun found annoying—lined up for her to mindblast one by one.

Now Folami laughed heartily. "*This* is how you plan to beat me, War Chief? I relived this moment the whole time I was in training, and I've done nothing *but* relive it ever since I was exposed to that gas of yours back on Oshun."

The stadium melted away, replaced with the rocky corridors of Olokun Station and the armored figure of Tobi in front of her.

"All you're doing is reminding me why I want to kill you."

"Fine," Tobi said. "No more subtlety."

Folami and Tobi had been exchanging psionic blasts. It was one of the first tricks Hembadoon had taught her, because it was so basic. All a telepath really did was stimulate the pain centers of the brain.

But what Tobi was doing right now was several orders of magnitude worse than anything Folami had learned from the Orisha. Every cell in her body felt as if it was on fire. Even her hair hurt.

She did not scream, however.

"You feel that, Ori-Inu?" Tobi was asking, no doubt *because* she didn't scream. "I figured I'd go for psychological pain, but that's a little harder than I figured. But hey, I'm flexible. You think that stupid Orisha taught you how to inflict this kind of pain?"

"No," Folami managed to say through clenched teeth.

"Yeah, I didn't think so. I'd love to keep this up, but we've only got another couple minutes before this station goes boom, so I think it's time I finished you off."

"You can try." Her answer to Tobi had not been a lie. She hadn't learned how to inflict *that* kind of pain.

But she had learned how to function while *feeling* that kind of pain.

So she was able to reach into the pocket of the coat. And then she was able to shrug off the coat and toss it toward Tobi.

The war chief looked down at the long leather coat that was

now right at his booted feet and smiled. "This is what you're reduced to, eh, Ori-Inu? Throwing your clothes at me? I'm going to enjoy—"

Whatever Tobi was going to enjoy was cut off by the explosion of the second grenade that Folami had in the pocket of Hembadoon's coat. She had feared that the coat would fall to the floor in such a way that the shaped charge would blow downward, but instead it was facing a direction that sent the blast right through Tobi's shins, tearing through his armor and the flesh and bone under it.

Tobi screamed in agony, and even as Folami's own pain subsided, she could feel the agony *he* suffered as the explosive splintered his shin bone, pulped the muscles in both legs, and utterly destroyed the war chief from the knees down.

Folami walked over to Tobi and stared him in the eye. Unable to stop her nose from twitching, she telekinetically raised Tobi's own Bayo to the man's face.

"Permission to disembark, War Chief?" she asked with a sweet smile before she mentally pulled the pistol's trigger and had it blow the top of Tobi's head off.

Then she turned and ran for the airlock. There was only another two-and-a-half minutes before Olokun exploded.

She arrived at the airlock to find Hembadoon standing outside it. "What—?"

"It's locked down," Hembadoon interrupted. "And you'll be *stunned* to learn that our priority won't override it."

"We don't need overrides," Folami said as she telekinetically forced the airlock door open.

She could feel the blood oozing out her nostrils, and her leg muscles felt like so much rubber. When she tried to walk into the airlock to board *Ebun*, she collapsed.

Luckily, Hembadoon was there to catch her. "It's okay, Folami," he said in a soothing voice that she last heard him use in the early days of training. "I got it from here."

Because she could read his mind, she knew that the thought was sincere. So she allowed herself to, at last, pass out.

EPILOGUE

ORANMIYAN SAT ALONE ON THE flight deck of *L'owuro.*

No. Not L'owuro. *That was Tobi's name. This is no longer a Hegemony ship.*

Right there, he decided to rename the vessel the *Abeje.* "You like that?" he asked the woman he named it after.

But no.

She was dead.

He finally had to admit to himself that Abeje was dead. When Olokun Station blew up, Folami probably died, too—he wasn't sure. He didn't feel her die, but *Abeje* was far enough from the asteroid when it exploded that he might not have.

And if Folami was alive? Well then Oranmiyan would probably have to kill her.

The dream was dead.

Time, he thought, to find a new dream.

Finally letting go of Abeje's corpse by setting it down amidst the dozen other corpses on the flight deck, Oranmiyan stood up and said, "Computer, set course for Orunmila."

When Folami woke up, she found herself sitting up against the bulkhead of *Ebun* and wearing another one of the Orisha's leather coats.

"Hembadoon?"

"Right here," he said from the vessel's only seat. "Sorry for dumping you on the deck, but we aren't exactly roomy in here."

"It's okay. How long was I out?"

"Approximately one hour."

She nodded. "I'm still exhausted."

"Hardly surprising, all things considered. We left in the proverbial nick of time. Olokun is just a bad memory, and we were far enough away to avoid any damage." He turned around to regard her with a serious expression. "Which leaves the question: where do we go from here?"

Folami blinked. Her instinctive response was to go back to Ife and report to Oba Isembi.

The same buruku *who authorized all those mindwipes during training, who sent me to Yemoja . . .*

But what else was she to do? For all that she now remembered her life on Oyo and during training on Ife, she was still an Ori-Inu, and she had a duty to report to her superior. For this mission, that superior was the Oba himself.

Of course, he was Hembadoon's superior, too. "Haven't you reported in?"

"I was waiting to discuss the matter with you. For one thing, I do not know the whole story—remember, while you were off gallivanting, I was tied to a bed."

"Right." Folami sighed. "I guess we should report in. Did anyone else get off the station?"

"*L'owuro* disembarked in plenty of time, but *Ebun* only read three life signs on board."

"Three?" That didn't make any sense. *L'owuro's* complement was for over a hundred. Even accounting for casualties on Oshun, there was no way the ship could have disengaged from the station with only three people on board.

"Are you sure the readings were right?"

Hembadoon nodded. "I checked one more time before they were too far away from Olokun to scan."

Letting out a long breath, Folami said, "Well, not much we can do about that. I guess—I guess we should report in."

"You don't want to." Hembadoon wasn't asking that as a question.

The response practically exploded out of Folami's mouth. "I don't know *what* I want to do! Everything's turned upside down!"

"So what's the alternative? Join the Oyo rebels?"

"Never," Folami said with utter disgust. Though she held Isembi and his Hegemony is plenty of contempt, it was as nothing compared to how she felt about the Oyo Empire, who whored out her mother to create a pet telepath for their god.

But where does that leave me? Where does any of this leave me?

"No," she said. "We report to the Oba."

"Very well, then. I'm setting course for Ifc."

She noticed that he wasn't activating the communications systems. "Shouldn't we contact the Oba first?"

"No. Let us give him the report in person." He smiled. "I think we've both earned some of Isembi's awful gin, don't you think?"

Folami smiled. "Fair enough, Orisha. Let's go."

The debris field created by the destruction sequence for Olokun Station left very little intact. The bodies, both living and dead, were pulverized. Identifying who was on the station when it exploded would require the use of a very fine DNA scanner.

Computer parts that weren't atomized were magnetized by the explosion. No information would be left in a single chip or circuit, if anyone could even find such a unit in anything like an intact condition.

But then there were the stasis chambers.

Designed by the best scientists that Tobi's money could buy, the stasis chambers were designed to survive an attack of much greater destructive capacity than the Olokun destruction sequence.

And so a half-dozen stasis chambers floated amidst the debris of Olokun Station, completely intact, and each occupied by a Nide.

Some of them began to wake up . . .

ABOUT THE AUTHOR

KEITH R.A. DeCANDIDO IS THE author more than forty-odd novels, a mess of short stories, a smattering of comic books, a bunch of novellas, and the occasional essay. His most recent work includes the novels *Unicorn Precinct*, the long-awaited sequel to his 2004 high fantasy police procedural *Dragon Precinct*, and *SCPD: The Case of the Claw*, first of a new series of novels about cops in a city filled with superheroes; short stories in the *Liar Liar, Tales from the House Band*, and *More Tales of Zorro* anthologies; the monthly *Farscape* comic book, written in collaboration with the TV series creator Rockne S. O'Bannon; and more. Coming in 2012 are *Goblin Precinct, Tales from Dragon Precinct,* and *SCPD: Avenging Amethyst*, as well as more stories of the Olodumare Hegemony for *The Scattered Earth*. Keith is also a black belt in *Kenshikai* karate, a contributor to the pop-culture podcast *The Chronic Rift* (www.chronicrift.com), the percussionist for the parody band Boogie Knights (www.boogie-knights.org), and a lifelong fan of the New York Yankees. You can listen to his twice-monthly podcast *Dead Kitchen Radio*, or go to www.DeCandido.net, which is a gateway to his blog (kradical.livejournal.com), his Facebook page (www.facebook.com/kradec), his Twitter feed (@KRADeC), and pretty much everything else.

ALSO FROM KEITH R. A. DECANDIDO

Get a peek at the first SCPD novel, *The Case of the Claw*!

PROLOGUE
SUNDAY

11.45PM

A yellow streak flew overhead, stirring up the litter on 20th Street. Officer Sean O'Malley didn't even notice it until the sonic boom rattled the windshield of the blue-and-white police car he was driving.

O'Malley steered the cruiser down 20th. From the seat next to him, Officer Paul Fiorello stuck his head out the window. "Was that Spectacular Man?"

Shaking his head and hitting the brake as the cruiser approached a red light at Jaffee Avenue, O'Malley said, "Christ, Paulie, how long you been livin' in this town? If it was him, it'd be blue and red. It was yellow, so that means the Flame."

This late on a Sunday night in the Simon Valley neighborhood, the streets were dark. Nothing was open, plus the street lights hadn't been repaired since the Bengal tangled with the Dread Gang last month.

"I can never remember," Fiorello said, "is he Ms. Terrific's brother or husband?" Flame and Ms. Terrific were two-thirds of the Terrific Trio.

O'Malley grinned as the light turned green and his foot moved from the brake to the accelerator. "Hope it's her brother, 'cause that lady's *hot*. I'd do her in a cold minute. Y'know, there's nude pictures of her on the Internet, right?"

"Gimme a break, Sean." Fiorello shook his head. "That's some skank they found at Bitches With No Brains dot com and Photoshopped the Terrific lady's head on it."

Frowning, O'Malley asked, "Seriously?"

Fiorello rolled his eyes. "Yeah. And Santa ain't real, either."

"Damn." O'Malley let out a long breath. They were some *fine* pictures.

"So yellow's Flame?" Fiorello started counting on his fingers. "Spec Man's, like you said, blue and red."

"Nice rhyme."

Fiorello gave O'Malley a nasty look before continuing. "So green's who? Major Marine?"

"Yeah. And purple's Amethyst and if it's all rainbow-y, then it's the Prism."

Shaking his head, Fiorello said, "I don't know how you keep track of the costumes like that."

"In this town, it's the job." O'Malley couldn't believe that his partner was still having trouble keeping it straight after all these years.

Fiorello's face looked sculpted: perfect Roman nose, dark hair that never got mussed no matter how crazy things got on the street, and friendly brown eyes that always calmed down the craziest of citizens. Which meant, of course, that women paid more attention to him than to O'Malley with his bad skin, messed-up nose thanks to an attempt to stop a bar brawl when he was a rookie, and crappy hair.

Still, Fiorello was good police, and he always had O'Malley's back—certainly more than the other assholes he'd been paired with over his six years on the job—so O'Malley put up with him as best he could.

Even if Fiorello always left Manny's with someone on his arm while O'Malley went home alone to an empty apartment.

The next street was Ayers, and O'Malley slowly turned the wheel to the right. Even on a Sunday night, there was always *something* happening on Ayers.

Sure enough, there was movement to O'Malley's left, as well as the sound of metal grinding against metal, though still no lighting. It was the Tavares Pawn Shop, which stayed open until midnight, though it looked like they were closing a few minutes early. The sound had come from a man pulling the grate shut; a woman was crouching down and pushing a padlock shut. O'Malley didn't know their first names, but he knew the Tavareses had always cooperated with the cops, reporting stolen merchandise and such.

Slowing down the cruiser, O'Malley leaned out the rolled-down window. "You guys all right?"

Mr. Tavares looked over and smiled when he saw the cops. "Yeah, we're good, Officer. Headin' home."

His wife, having applied both padlocks, stood upright. "Hey, guys, if you see the Bruiser tonight, could you do me a favor and thank him? Some guy tried to jump me on the way in to open this morning, and he drove 'im off."

"If we see him," O'Malley muttered. "Get home safe."

"Thanks!"

"What the hell?" Fiorello asked as they continued down Ayers. "'If we see him'? Sounds like DeLaHoya saved her ass."

"I guess."

Fiorello stared at his partner. "C'mon, DeLaHoya's one of the good guys. And you know how I know that? YOU said it when we first partnered up. 'Most 'a the costumes,' you said, 'they're assholes, but the Bruiser's okay.' So what the hell?"

O'Malley sighed. "You know that double MacAvoy caught last week? DeLaHoya fucked with the evidence—they had to toss the case 'cause 'a him."

Fiorello shook his head. "He doesn't usually do that."

"Yeah, well, he ain't police. None 'a them are." O'Malley went through an intersection, ignoring the octagonal stop sign.

His heart suddenly hammered into his chest as he saw a square block of a man dressed all in black jump into the middle of the street right in the cruiser's path.

"Dammit!" O'Malley slammed on the brakes and tried to get his breathing under control. It wouldn't do to run down the Bruiser, since in that confrontation, the costume would still be standing, and the front grille of the blue-and-white would be smashed in. The last thing O'Malley wanted to do was call in a damaged cruiser *again*—not after that time the Brute Squad totaled the unit, and he had to ride a desk for a week.

Fiorello smirked. "Hey, now you can give him the Tavares lady's message."

"Kiss my ass," O'Malley said.

No one knew what exactly happened to Jesus DeLaHoya to make him super-strong, invulnerable, and big as a house, but ever since it happened, the former amateur boxer—who'd acquired the nickname of "the Bruiser" when he was a Gold Gloves champ back in the day—had taken it upon himself to clean up Simon Valley. Unlike most of the costumes, he usually cooperated with the cops, and even testified in court when he helped put someone away.

DeLaHoya walked around to the driver's side. The verb *to walk* was probably not giving what he did enough credit. The Bruiser tended to stomp, on account of he weighed a ton, and O'Malley was just waiting for the day that the pavement gave out under him and he fell into the sewer.

"Officers, how you two doin'?" the Bruiser said. He was bending over and staring into the window at O'Malley, getting so close that he could smell the cheap coffee on the costume's breath. DeLaHoya kept his dark hair close cropped, and it just accentuated that his head looked like a trapezoid, with no noticeable neck—just went straight from the jaw line to the shoulders.

"Whaddaya want?" O'Malley asked.

"Got somethin' you two'll wanna see."

O'Malley looked at Fiorello. "You believe this?" He turned back to the costume. "Look, DeLaHoya—"

"It's *serious*." With that, the Bruiser stood upright and stomped toward an alley between two apartment buildings.

Fiorello got out of the car.

"Hey, Paulie, what the hell?" O'Malley asked, but his partner was already crossing in front of the blue-and-white to follow the costume.

Shaking his head, O'Malley said, "Fine." He turned off the ignition and got out, pulling his ballcap out of his back pocket and putting it on his head. Technically, the plain black ballcap wasn't proper uniform, but O'Malley had always hated the blue department-issue hat. Fiorello, of course, wore his, with the SCPD logo on the front and the word central under it—and it never messed up his hair. O'Malley really had no idea how he did it.

Adjusting the bill of the cap as he walked toward the alley, O'Malley asked, "You wanna give us a hint, DeLaHoya?"

"I got a tip that some of Turk's boys were dealin' outta here."

This was starting to annoy O'Malley as he followed his partner and the Bruiser, pulling out his flashlight so he could see. "Turk's boys been dealin' outta here forever." His nose started to wrinkle, as the alley smelled like half a dozen homeless guys had taken a shit and then all croaked. O'Malley started breathing through his mouth.

"Not the last six months, they ain't," the Bruiser said, and O'Malley could hear the pride in his voice. "So I was checkin' it out, and I found this."

The Bruiser and Fiorello had stopped walking, the costume pointing between two Dumpsters. O'Malley shined his flashlight where the Bruiser's meaty finger was aimed, and Fiorello did likewise.

Barely, O'Malley could tell that it was the body of a man—and then only because the face was more or less intact. The rest of the body, though, had been torn apart. Organs and bones were sticking up through ripped flesh and torn clothes, and blood was all over everything. The limbs, what he could see of them, were all pointed in different directions than legs and arms usually went.

Something was stuck on the man's forehead.

The light got dimmer, and O'Malley turned to see Fiorello run across to the other side of the alley to throw up. He almost made it. His retching echoed off the brick walls of the two buildings. Uncharitably, O'Malley wondered what all those women who ignored him and chased Fiorello would think if they saw the two of them right now.

O'Malley shined his flashlight directly on the victim's forehead. It was a yellow Post-It with a pen-and-ink drawing of an eagle's talon on it.

The Bruiser said, "That's what I think it is, right?"

Nodding, O'Malley said, "Yeah." He turned and flashed his light on Fiorello, who was still doubled over, and was now dry heaving. His regurgitated dinner was doing nothing to make the alley smell better. "Guess *I'm* callin' this in."

"Look, I still gotta find Turk's boys. Can you just say this was an anonymous tip or something?"

"You didn't touch nothin', right?"

The Bruiser sighed. "Look, I'm sorry about what happened. That was a mistake, and I already apologized to Detective MacAvoy—twice. I didn't touch *anything*, okay?"

O'Malley was about to argue some more, but there wasn't any point. Besides, he now had bigger problems. "Yeah, fine, go beat the shit outta Turk's boys. Oh, and hey—Mrs. Tavares, from the pawn shop? She says thanks."

At that, the Bruiser actually broke into a big grin, which made his ugly face even uglier. "Tell her she's welcome." And then he stomped back out of the alley.

Fiorello was now standing with his hands on his knees, dry heaving. O'Malley grabbed the radio that was clipped to his right shoulder. "PCD, this is Unit 2202 with a signal 85. We got a dead body in the alley on the 400 block of Ayers. Need crime scene and Homicide."

"PCD roger."

"And hey, PCD?" O'Malley looked down at the mangled corpse and the distinctive Post-It. "Tell Homicide that the Claw's back."

Also From the Tales of the Scattered Earth
Read a sample chapter of The Second Veil,
by David Nial Wilson

CHAPTER ONE

THE MAIN CHAMBER OF THE meeting hall of The High Council of Urv was a stately edifice with towering columns and a decorated, vaulted ceiling. It was centered by a huge oval table of polished stone and ringed with ornate chairs covered in plush upholstery. It was, in fact, a statement, and as Euphrankes Holmynn entered, all he could do was shake his head.

Seated around that table, watching his entrance in solemn silence, an array of gray-haired councilmen waited in frowning silence. Euphrankes had been in the chamber before, and he'd known, more or less, what to expect, but the sheer pomposity of it still made him cringe.

The walls were hung with portraits of still more elders. They dated back to the beginning of The Council. When Euphrankes, as a boy, had asked what there had been before the earliest portrait, he'd been cuffed on the ear and told to keep his silence. He had since come to understand that he'd gotten his answer . . . they didn't know.

The rule for all those summoned to The High Council Chamber was silence. There were words to be spoken, but though they called it a court, there were no deliberations to be made. There were lines on old parchment that spoke with the voice of the law, and policy never deviated. That is why, stepping into the center of the room, where a slightly raised circular stage stood facing the base end of The Council table, seemed like such a waste of time and a display of idiocy. Euphrankes already knew what they would say.

It didn't matter. He'd made his request because it was his nature to make such requests. He'd stood his ground because he knew that he was not the only man on the planet who wished that things might change—that it was possible to prove the limitations and proclamations of law were not inviolate. It didn't even really matter that they would say no, because he knew that—in the end—there would come a time when it didn't matter what they thought, or what they said. If he died in the attempt, he would die knowing in his heart what was, and was not, the truth.

The chamber was only dimly lit by a ring of flickering lanterns. The only bright spot was where he stood, a trick of lenses and mirrors, and he knew this was to make it difficult for him to meet their gaze or study their expressions, while making it simple for them to do the same to him. Euphrankes' father had helped in the most recent redesign of the chamber, and he still had the books of notes explaining the structure, construction, and purpose of each architectural tidbit.

It was, in fact, the influence of his father, Edwin, that allowed Euphrankes to be granted any audience at all. He knew that he was a disappointment to The Council. His father had done great things at their bidding. His inventions and his innovations, as well as many of the technologies behind the existing infrastructure of the city, had made their lives easier. Euphrankes, rather than proving helpful, had done little in his life but cause them a long string of headaches for which the only cure had proven a semi-banishment to a private dome outside the city. He wondered grimly where they might send him next if he angered them sufficiently.

A phlegmy cough broke the silence, and Euphrankes stood as calmly as he could, facing the length of the table. It stretched interminably into the distance, and at the far end, in a dim pool of illumination, High Councilor Cumby sat and gazed back at him. At least, Euphrankes assumed the High Councilor was looking at him. At such a distance he might have been asleep, or facing the opposite way entirely.

"Good morning, Euphrankes," Cumby said. Despite the distance, the acoustics of the chamber amplified the old man's voice so that it seemed the two were standing side by side.

Euphrankes bowed very slightly and kept his expression as devoid of emotion as possible. He didn't believe there was any chance of his request being approved, but he didn't want to give them new reason for their denial before they'd even spoken it.

"It is an honor, as always," Euphrankes said.

"Is it indeed?" Cumby asked. "Well, we shall see. I would like to extend my condolences on the loss of your father. He was a great man. He will be sorely missed in the city, and in these chambers. I pray that his passing was a gentle one."

"It was," Euphrankes said. He was surprised at how close his voice came to breaking as he spoke those words. His father *had* been a great man in the city, but the man Euphrankes remembered—the brilliant mind that had shown him the magic of metal and gears, steam and pressure, mathematics and theory—had been the rock in his life. His father had kept him busy and sane when he'd wanted to rail against The Council and their rules.

"One of the last things he said to me," Euphrankes added, trying to be as politic as possible, "was that I should send his regards to this council. I've chosen to carry them personally, and hope that you will forgive the indulgence."

A soft murmur ran about the table at his words. Euphrankes figured they were nodding and patting one another on the back. They'd always believed his father to be their tool—a man who would do as he was bid and give no argument. So unlike his son.

In truth, for every project Edwin Holmynn had completed for The Council, he'd completed a dozen others in the streets, taking care of those in need, and studying ways and means to move beyond the stagnant, dying city he'd called home. When a small outlying branch of the veil-roads had become untenable, it was Edwin who, through judicious use of his influence and several daring trips by air, between veils, had salvaged the complex to which his son had been banished. It was as if he'd glanced into the future and prepared a safe haven against the inevitable.

None of that mattered now. What mattered was that the city was dying, and these old fools didn't care. They would be perfectly content to sit back and watch, their laws fiercely clutched in liver-spotted, blue-veined hands, as the city shrank around them, becoming in the end a mass coffin. None of them had that many years of life left, and an equal number of them cared for the well-being of the inhabitants of Urv living beyond their immediate circle of acquaintance.

"We welcome you," the High Councilor said at last. "We are informed that you have a request, and we are . . . eager . . . to hear what you have in mind. Your family has always served the needs of The Council, and of the city."

Again, Euphrankes gave his small, half bow. Then he stood to his full six foot four inches and squared his shoulders. He was a big man with a slender, muscular frame tapering to powerful shoulders. His hair was long, and he wore it back over his shoulders in a braid, as his father had before him. He knew that they could hear him if he spoke softly, but he chose to project. He wanted to catch them sleeping and maybe, just maybe jostle them awake long enough to win their support.

"As you know," he said, "the roads between the cities are becoming steadily more treacherous. Flights beyond the First Veil run at regular intervals now, carrying cargo and passengers. Still, they are serving a shrinking world."

There were cleared throats and coughs around the room. Euphrankes held his temper in check, and continued.

"It isn't just the cities. The outlying factories and agricultural collectives are failing. Power sources are limited, and the rituals do not always work to repair what has fallen to age or neglect. It is a troubling time."

"Have you come," a voice piped up from his left, "to lecture us on the history of our world, young man?"

Illana Mirkos, eldest of the women serving on The Council, was a shrill, overbearing woman who had never forgiven Euphrankes' father for turning down her offer of marriage. It would have elevated Euphrankes' family to a level where they might—one day—hold a seat on The Council, but Illana had been twenty years his father's senior, and she was insufferable. She was least likely of all the members of The Council to look favorably upon anything Euphrankes proposed.

"No lady," he said, turning to acknowledge her, but unwilling to be cut off before he'd spoken his peace. "I am here talking about our future, and whether, in fact, there is to be such a future if we do not soon take action to ensure it. The prophets predict another ten years might bring a time when there is no ground travel between cities at all; how long can our cities exist without fuel, or food? Our present fleet of airships cannot bear the brunt of such a catastrophe."

"And you have a solution?" High Councilor Cumby cut in. "I assume by your prattle that this is why you are here. You have some way to prevent the roads from crumbling, or to tie the cities one to the other?"

Euphrankes paused. This was the critical moment. What he proposed was actually not intended to help with the roads. It would not, in fact, make moving supplies from one city to another simpler or cheaper. His vision was more far-reaching than that of The Council, and the moment to show that divergence was upon him.

"I have developed a means," he said, ignoring the question and thus dodging the answer, "to travel beyond the Second Veil. The resources of this planet are finite. We lack the material or facilities to repair or rebuild what has fallen. We must look outward, not inward for a solution. We must look beyond the Second Veil, and I have created a ship that . . ."

Several voices rang out at once. They ranged from high-pitched screeching to angry shouts. High Councilor Cumby glared across the expanse of the table to where Euphrankes stood, letting the tumult grow until the room reverberated with the cacophony, then slammed his hand down on a button embedded in the tabletop. A piercing shriek of sound emanated from amplifying tubes around the room. The vibration of the sound met in the center of the room and swirled, swallowing all the words and screams and protests completely. When Cumby released the button, the room was heavy with silence, and

Euphrankes stood, his shoulders shaking with startled anger and outrage.

"You dare?" Cumby said. The old man actually rose from his seat at council, a thing Euphrankes had never witnessed.

"I . . ."

Suddenly whatever it was that amplified Euphrankes' voice died, and though he continued to stutter into the void, only the High Councilor's voice could be heard.

"You dare to come before this council and suggest that, not only are the laws and the prophecies to be ignored, but that the very safety of our planet should be violated? You dare to suggest," the old man paused and seemed to gasp for the breath he needed before plunging on, "that we cause the very type of damage we fear every waking moment of every day?"

Euphrankes took a hesitant step backward, nearly toppling from the speaker's platform. He had been caught completely off guard by this attack. He'd known they would not condone his research, but this?

"Your Honors," he said softly.

No one heard him.

"You will leave this chamber," Cumby roared, his voice gathering strength from some unknown and unsuspected source, "and you will not return. You will cease any research you have begun toward this blasphemy. You will bend your efforts to clearing the roads and repairing the veils, or by all that is holy, I will forget my respect for your father, and I will have you cast out."

The silence, if possible, grew thicker at these words. It was one thing to be banished to an outer sphere, where he was cut off from all normal road traffic in and out of the city. It was quite another to be released from the veil into the outer atmosphere of their world. It was far too thin to sustain life, and it was a punishment not meted out in the forty-two years of Euphrankes' life. It was a sentence of death thinly cloaked in false charity.

He turned. Without another word, features rigid and limbs so stiff he felt each step jolt through his frame as if he pounded his bare feet on concrete, he turned and walked away from The Council table. He stared straight ahead, and when he reached the air lock he stepped inside. Two guards stood beside the door to ensure he did not try to return to the chamber. Euphrankes heard the soft hiss of equalizing pressure. As the doors closed he heard the shriek of the High Councilor's silence reverberating through the room once more. He wondered briefly what they had to argue about, now that his humiliation was complete, but could spare it no concentration. The time for talking was behind him, and he knew what he had to do.

"Sorry, father," he whispered.

Then the outer portal opened, and he stepped into the stale, slightly thinner air of the street and turned toward a series of tall, imposing towers.

The city was a series of low-slung, rectangular buildings stacked neatly, like a child's blocks, one atop the other. A quick glance gave the impression that the city was one big, continuous structure, but it was misleading. There were walls and boundaries within each building. Everything was built in layers, and each of those layers was—in one way or another—sealed off from all others.

Gleaming metal conduits wound up and around the walls, climbed over the roof tops and joined at huge, hydraulically activated valves. The buildings were all closed loops of breathable air, filtered and re-constituted. Near the edge of the veil, generators hummed and hissed as they sucked sustenance from the planet beyond, just enough chemicals and gases and droplets of moisture to sustain the system and prevent them from choking on their own exhaust. It reminded Euphrankes of the machines sometimes used to keep medical patients alive and breathing when their bodies began to fail.

As he walked, he felt the city closing in around him with claustrophobic, breath-stealing power. Ahead were the airship towers. Each served as a dock for one or two ships, magnetic plates holding the great vessels in position just above the First Veil. The locks—seams in the veil surrounded by special vacuum seals on either side—were located beneath each berth.

The *Vector* hovered where he'd left her, and Euphrankes made for the lock leading up to his ship with a purpose. He'd never seen The Council so worked up, and was only glad there had been no time for Myril, the High Priest of The Temple, to get involved. There had been no one cast from the city in a very long time—but if there was one on The Council who would relish the opportunity to bring that age-old punishment back into the mainstream of the cities daily life—it was Myril.

Euphrankes reached the bottom rung of the ladder leading up to his platform, and began to climb. As he made his way up, he glanced over at the one structure in the city of Urv taller than The Council chambers. The Temple of the Veils, while as sealed and impregnable as any other building in Urv, had a gleaming white façade of stone and a massive airlock chamber that had once allowed an entire congregation of worshipers to enter at one time. The clang of those huge doors closing had rung like a great bell as they sealed off the faithful. They had remained closed for nearly a decade, but Euphrankes remembered that sound from his childhood, and he shuddered. It had always sounded to him like the doors of a great tomb closing.

On the platform above, two attendants nodded in recognition. One, a tow-headed boy with a big grin, snapped a quick salute.

Euphrankes took a deep breath, expelled it, and willed his anger and frustration to join the stale, filtered air. He managed a wry grin.

"I'm taking off immediately," he called out. "Give me five."

The boy nodded, and Euphrankes entered the bottom lock, which sealed quickly behind him. When the seal was complete, he climbed up through the membrane-like portal to the upper lock, and waited for it to seal behind him. Then, operating the upper lock manually by means of a wheel, he lowered the pressure inside to match the thin, anemic air of the outer atmosphere, and climbed quickly through. He turned, spun the wheel tight, and mounted the dangling rope ladder to The *Vector*.

Above him, Aria had already opened the outer lock. He smiled. Even though it was much more difficult to catch his breath, the sensation of freedom that stole over him each time he left the lower levels behind buoyed his spirits. He climbed, pacing himself and conserving his breath. He didn't want to become lightheaded. If he fell, the odds were not good that he'd recover enough to climb again, or that Aria could get a lift down to him before he suffocated. He could have worn a suit, but he'd always preferred the risk—and the exhilaration—of facing the air beyond the First Veil on his own terms.

He reached the air lock, pulled himself up the last few feet, and closed the hatch. Immediately, fresh air, purified and drawn from beyond the lower veil by his own pumps, flooded the chamber. A moment later he popped his head up through the main hatch and called out without preamble.

"Cast off and get me away from this place."

He closed the hatch, sealed it carefully, and turned toward the bridge. The *Vector* was a large, sleek craft, the largest of its type ever built. His father had begun construction before his death, and Euphrankes had completed the work, adding a number of improvements to the initial design.

The ship worked on very simple principles. The main structure was surrounded by a thick membrane similar in function to the veils on the planet. These membranes were filled with a gas his father had named "Freethion," which was considerably lighter even than the thin air beyond the First Veil. The lightness was caused, in some arcane manner, by a reaction to gravity itself rather than physical weight. The lift was so powerful, in fact, that it was only through the employment of electromagnetic "anchors" that they were able to prevent the ship from shooting skyward and bursting through the upper veil. The magnets also provided steering, as the surface of the planet was rich with iron.

Euphrankes settled into the pilot's seat as Aria made her way around the bridge releasing each anchor in turn. He watched her, and his mood lightened again. She was a slender woman, tall and lithe, dressed in the loose, comfortable clothing of an engineer. She hadn't accompanied him into the city for a number of reasons, not the least of which was her disdain for any attire The Council or temple would deem "appropriate." Her hair hung in dark rivulets over one shoulder, where she'd tied it in the center with a strip of leather.

The two had been companions for more than a decade, ever since she'd come to him to learn the science of the airships. Her family had been cut off from Urv when one of the roadways began losing pressure. Both ends had been sealed, and the only way left between the two cities was through the veils. She'd been a quick student, and though they'd made several trips to visit her parents in Mancea, each time she'd returned. It was the best business arrangement he'd ever made.

The *Vector* was as different from the Chamber of The High Council as Euphrankes could make it. The crew seats were leather. The benches were wood, but though it was sanded smooth and carefully tooled, it was utilitarian. The metal was polished, but it served a purpose. Nothing was frivolous or wasted.

They could fly the ship with only the two of them, but it was designed for a crew of six on extended trips. They had only a couple of hour's flight to and from Urv, so they'd come alone. Aria crossed the bridge, watching the lines and positioning magnets. They steered by the stars at night, and by landmarks by day. The damaged roads between the cities and outposts were easy to spot, even from a great height, and made navigation a simple matter of connecting the dots. The *Vector* was tuned to their habits and their comfort, and the two were more at home on her bridge than they'd ever been in their laboratory, or the city.

Aria set the course, and turned back to him, coming to stand by his side. The front of the ship was a great, thick window, round and spoked with metal reinforced beams. As they gained speed, leaving the city and The Council behind, she said, "So, I take it things did not go well with The Council."

Euphrankes swatted at her playfully and she darted away, laughing.

"I think," he said, settling back, "that The Council and I have finally parted ways."

"It's about time," she said, returning to lean in and kiss him deeply. "I was afraid you were getting boring."

"That," he said, "is the one thing you never have to worry about."

She settled into his lap, and he held her, enjoying the closeness and the warmth, and staring up and out of the domed glass portal into the distant stars.

Curious about other Crossroad Press books?
Stop by our site:
http://store.crossroadpress.com
We offer quality writing
in digital, audio, and print formats.

Enter the code FIRSTBOOK
to get 20% off your first order from our store!
Stop by today!